FLORRY
of
WASHINGTON HEIGHTS

FLORRY
of
WASHINGTON HEIGHTS

A Novel by Steve Katz

Sun & Moon Press
LOS ANGELES

Cover: Photograph by Steve Katz
Design: Katie Messborn
Publication of this book was made possible, in part, through a grant
from the National Endowment for the Arts and through contributions
to The Contemporary Arts Educational Project, Inc., a non-profit
corporation.

The New American Fiction Series: 10

Library of Congress Cataloguing in Publication Data

Katz, Steve, 1935
    Florry of Washington Heights

ISBN: 0-940650-83-5
ISBN: 0-930650-84-3 (pbk.)
ISBN: 0-930650-85-1 (signed)

FIRST EDITION
10 9 8 7 6 5 4 3 2 1

Sun & Moon Press
6363 Wilshire Blvd., Suite 115
Los Angeles, CA 90048

Also by Steve Katz

The Exagggerations of Peter Prince
Creamy and Delicious
Posh
Cheyenne River Wild Track
The Lestriad
The Weight of Antony
Moving Parts
Stolen Stories
Wier & Pouce

FLORRY
of
WASHINGTON HEIGHTS

Whoever tells you he knows everything about his own neighborhood you can be sure is fooling himself. Something else always goes on in the schoolyard while you sit on the park wall, or vice versa. When I was a kid, I learned that. So when I grew up I never expected to understand all the world, not even with all the education I could get, not even as a lawyer. So now I'm never shocked at anything that happens, and I'm not too disappointed if I can't do much about it. To have the illusion that you can understand the world you've got to come from a small town. That's why astronauts don't hail from New York City. If a New Yorker rides up on a space shot, he looks down and says, "Big deal. Turn it over and let's see the rest of it." An astronaut comes from Berrien Springs or White Lake, someplace like that, where gossip is in control. That's where someone believes that everything to be known is known. That's the power of gossip. That's where yakkers keep the records. A guy from Muncie, Indiana, sees one side of the planet and assumes the other side is there. Not a New Yorker. What they call the "know-it-all attitude" is no one knows anything. It's all up for grabs. Look the other way. A Puerto Rican opens the hood of his burned-out Chrysler and all his roosters fly out, and nobody notices. Why should they? Chickens in a Chrysler. Big deal. I've seen that happen. They were fighting chickens.

But a neighborhood is not altogether unlike a small town. This one had a park in it, with a wall you could sit on. It had a public school with a schoolyard. It had Broadway in it with candystores and drugstores and hardware stores, a couple of movie theaters, a camera shop, a Chinese restaurant, a Greek restaurant, a Y attached to a synagogue, some churches, groceries, fruitstands, bakeries, butchers. The George Washington Bridge was attached to this neighborhood, and that went clear to Jersey, where there were several small towns. We were like a small town in that a lot of the people knew each other, especially the kids. We were tight. We were gangs; that is, some of us were gangs, some of us were social and athletic clubs, which meant mainly baseball, basketball, and girls, not necessarily in that order, but according to the season.

When I first saw *West Side Story* it reminded me that such things happened probably in every neighborhood, certainly in Washington Heights, though not so romantic, so pretty, so "Romeo and Juliet." Every neighborhood has its own story that deserves to be told, and I thought that some day I would tell mine. So here it is.

My gang was the New York Bullets Social and Athletic Club. We had purple and gold reversible jackets—wool on one side, satin on the other—our names embroidered above the heart on each side, and BULLETS across the back on the gold side, and a big terrycloth B opposite the name on the purple side. In case you wonder about my name, it was Swanny on the jacket—Swanson—though now that I'm a lawyer they call me William, or my friends call me Bill, or my partners W.S. My clients who've seen me work like to call me B.S. We weren't fighters, not like the Condors or the Fanwoods, who enjoyed to kick ass more than anything. I could never understand that. More than making out with girls. More than getting to play in Yankee Stadium for the American Legion finals, which we almost did once. The Fanwoods were mostly Irish and they lived on the other side of Broadway, the Harlem River side, as did the Condors, except they lived mostly above 178th Street, and they were more Italian. The Bullets were mostly Jewish, except for Stamatakis and Zoo who were Greek, and Mamoulian who said he was Armenian, but he was like a Jewish guy too. I was the only Irish guy. Half Irish. My mother was Jewish from the Lower East Side, and my dad was Irish; I mean, real Irish. Married my mother a year after he got here from the old sod, and I was born a year after that, in the middle of the depression. He was a tinker, like an Irish gypsy, and he still earned his living with the people of his tribe, a lot of whom lived in the South, like South Carolina, and they had a barn-painting scam. They'd travel around and stop at people's farms and convince them that their barns needed painting. They'd always say they had some paint left over from their last job, and give them what sounded like a good price, then paint the barn with this watered-down stuff that washed off in the next rain. He was gone five months of the year doing that, and he came back with enough money for rent, and we ate good. He never talked about that, and I didn't find out about this life of his till after he died. My dad liked living in New York City, for the cultural advantages. He was a poet, but I didn't know it. Like I said, you can't know everything. I found his notebooks after he died.

Anyway, the neighborhood was Washington Heights in

Manhattan, up by the George Washington Bridge. Probably the most famous guy so far to come out of that neighborhood was Henry Kissinger. He was before the Bullets, however, so we never got to see him play baseball, though I had a feeling about him once I found out he was from the neighborhood that he was probably just like Ginzy the Creep, who always hung around the schoolyard or the park, waiting to be chosen into the game, and he never got in, and if he did it was to play right field, and it was because his mother had brought him to the schoolyard to make sure little Henry got to play. That's what he always looked like to me in the White House—like a kid surprised he'd been chosen into the game. He's a fake-out. That's someone who makes his bucks or gets his position on a foundation of lies, particularly lies about himself. To anyone from my neighborhood Kissinger was an obvious fake-out. He makes the mistake of acting like he understands the whole world, like I said you couldn't do if you come from the city. But you get the idea that he really knows he doesn't, and he's smart, because he's pretending, because he likes to ride the jets and eat in the hundred dollar fancy restaurants, with the *haut monde*. I get this from his voice. It makes me want to vomit. It's a voice that seems to gurgle up from the sewers. I mean, I'm a liar, because I'm a lawyer, and I've got my scams like my father had; but that guy lies to himself.

So just when you think you're beginning to know your neighborhood, you've got things figured out and you're safe, something happens. Someone shows up to change your ideas, especially when you're a kid, because a kid knows everything, and what he doesn't know doesn't interest him. That's why Sugarman's romance was a shock to all of us and a turning point for all the Bullets in the neighborhood.

A lot of us sat around on the park wall between 174th and 175th streets when the weather was decent and generally we bullshitted, and if one of us had a basketball we dribbled it, passed it behind our backs, all that. It was right near Barney's newsstand where we hung out, which was at the 175th Street station for the A train. Barney was fifty-five or sixty at the time, and he ran that stand with his wife where they sold newspapers and candy bars. They never had any kids of their own, so they enjoyed having us hang around, particularly since we were the Bullets and peaceloving, most of us smart kids probably headed for college. He knew us all from when we were real little during World War II, when there was a bubble gum shortage, and he'd always somehow have a box of Dubble-Bubble under the counter, or Bazooka, and he'd save it for us—a couple of pieces a week at a dime a shot—which for most of us at seven or eight years old was a week's allowance. At the time we thought it was a bargain, and in fact Dufner would buy from Barney at a dime and sell for a quarter in school. Barney made a good profit on us. He and his wife retired to Fort Lauderdale in 1956 or so, and now his little wooden stand is gone, as is Dubble-Bubble and Bazooka, and the lust we had for chewing it.

We hung out at Barney's because we were a little paranoid and he had a telephone. They hadn't come yet, but the Fanwoods could come around any time they felt like beating up some Jews. Some of them went to this Incarnation school where the fathers and nuns taught them that the Jews killed Christ so any time they wanted to have some fun, the rumor went, they'd go out and stomp some Jews and feel good about it. I'm saying it hadn't happened yet, but we felt safer close to Barney's telephone. One quick call to Schletzbaum's father at the 42nd Precinct would bring a couple of squad cars down Fort Washington Avenue to cool things off. The Fanwoods had respect for the police, because they were Irish. The Condors didn't have that respect. They were like mafia hitters in training. Beating up Bullets wasn't much training for them. They weren't much interested in Jews. No challenge. Not like going up to 207th Street. Not like unloading some muscle on the legendary Barons of Inwood.

"Sit on this and rotate," Dufner gave the finger to the number five bus running downtown. "I hate that bus driver."

"So what's your father gonna do about it? What has he got, a prick stretcher or something?" Bernie Grossman was talking to Booby Oserow about Booby's male implement, Booby's favorite topic of conversation.

"No," Dufner interrupted. He loved to be a pain in the ass. He had little else to recommend him. "He's gonna take your little sister home and put it in her mouth."

"Lay off my little sister." Bernie was sensitive about his sister, who was a year younger and pretty, and already liked boys too much.

"We all know she loves to suck dick."

"Hey, you're cruisin' for a bruise."

"You don't like it you can lump it." Dufner stretched his chin out at Grossman. I was holding the basketball, and I threw it into Dufner's gut.

"Lay off."

He caught the basketball. "Lay off your mother." He bounced the ball over the park wall, into the bushes.

"Get the ball," I said. Frankie Dufner wasn't an easy kid to like.

"You sit on this and rotate," he gave me the finger. There

was something really mean, repressed, and angry about him. He dropped out of Hunter College after a year, and now he has a store in Little Italy; sells weapons, uniforms, bulletproof vests, flashlights, badges to the cops.

"Get the ball," I repeated and stared at him, and I didn't have to say anything else.

"Your mother," he mumbled, and jumped over the wall to get my basketball.

"He's gonna use hormones. He's got hormones to give me," said Booby Oserow.

"Did you ever hear a hormone?" Dufner shouted from the other side of the wall.

"Hormones?" Bernie said. "Hormones to make your putz grow? Your father's a dentist." He was only fourteen and a half like the rest of us, but was already worried about what to do when he got to be a grown-up, and he figured what someone does is what someone is. A dentist is in the mouth, he figures.

"So he's a dentist," said Booby. "Your father works in the subways. That doesn't mean he can't take a bus." Booby was a really fat kid, obese you'd say, and he was a Bullet just to be a Bullet, just to hang out with us, though he never played baseball or basketball with us, only if we were really desperate. We all liked him, even though he was obsessed with his little petzel under all those rolls of fat. A lot of us went to his father for a dentist, who was fat and funny himself, and collected French decks and sunbathing magazines. Sometimes Booby would hide some under his shirt and bring them to school. His father had this ancient X-ray machine that gives me cancer just to remember it. It sparked like one of those space ships on Captain Video, and he loved to take X-rays, and never used anything to shield himself or his patients. He died pretty young, his fat body blossoming with tumors, his fat Booby managing at the time the Nedicks store on 42nd Street and 8th Avenue.

"So you think girls like boys with a big prick?" Bernie Grossman asked. "How big is a pussy? Wouldn't it hurt them?"

"It's as big as your mouth," said Frankie Dufner, practicing a dribble between his legs.

"Hey Cousy," I said, motioning for him to throw me the ball.

"It can get gigantic." Zohos was the Greek kid we called Zoo. He looked eighteen at least. He could have already grown a moustache with the hair on his face. "I mean your big head had to come out of one of them. Think about it." Everyone was thinking. Zoo played center field for us, because he was the one who looked most like Joe DiMaggio, and he moved pretty good under a fly ball on his long legs. His number was 5 on his jacket, like Joltin' Joe's. Mine was 15 because I admired Tommy Henrich, old reliable. That's the way I always thought about myself even when I was a kid—never spectacular, always reliable. Zoo hit pretty good for percentage, but he didn't hit the long ball like Stamatakis, our other Greek, a mountainous kid. Stames could clear the fence.

"If she's hot," Zoo went on. His voice was deep, resonant, and always sounded like he knew what he was talking about, and he looked like he could know all about girls. He went to school out West in Indiana and later became a TV newscaster, though I still think of him as a pharmacist. "It's like a boner inside out, if she's hot. But bigger. The hotter the bigger. You get her hot, that's the boy's job."

"What if she clamps up?" I asked. That was always my secret fear.

"How do you know how big it gets?" Bernie asked Zoo.

"He put it in your sister," Dufner taunted him again.

"Oh yeah?" Grossman swelled up to his full five foot three and stepped into Dufner's square of sidewalk and looked right in his face. "Oh yeah?"

"Except if she clamps up," I said again, to remind everyone of that danger, because once she does it, I thought, she has you as long as she wants you. You're caught like a dog. You're attached to her and she can get up and answer the door and you're still there. She can drag you along and show you to her mother.

"You're still cruisin' for a bruise, Dufner." Grossman pushed him.

Dufner wasn't a fighter. He could provoke a fight, and he was a snitch. He'd hold your coat if you were going to fight, but when it came to his own physical body, he avoided bruises. He'd exert psychological pressure. He'd talk his way into the background.

"Juicy Lucy," he said to Grossman. Behind his back we all called Grossman's sister Juicy. Dufner backed off and jumped up to sit on the wall.

"Hey," said Booby. "Damn. Hey, look at that." Booby was pointing across the street. We all looked.

"Zoom," said Dufner, slipping off the wall. "Bang. Zoom. And away we go."

Those were the last words said for several minutes. Across the street was a Bullet jacket, gold side out, slowly strolling. There was Fred Sugarman, our shortstop and baseball captain. He was strolling too, but he wasn't wearing the jacket. A girl was wearing the jacket, and all of us recognized her, and that's why we shut up. They weren't holding hands, but they walked close enough together so we could tell that during the course of their stroll they had been. What was most serious was that she was wearing his jacket. To wear a guy's jacket meant everything. It was a step beyond going steady. It was just an inch before being engaged for a kid almost fifteen. And this was the first Bullet jacket ever worn by a girl. Of course we'd had them only for a couple of months, and we talked a lot about the kind of girls we'd let wear our jackets; but, to tell you the truth, none of us had had the opportunity yet, though a few months later Juicy Lucy talked Zoo out of his jacket for a couple of weeks, and Dufner actually lost his jacket, and maybe his virginity too, to Audrey Wolfe who was seventeen or more. He never saw his jacket again, and as he said he didn't care. He got something. She got something. "I'm quitting the Bullets anyway," he said. But Sugarman's jacket was the first, and the girl wearing it was, by general consensus, the prettiest girl in the neighborhood. I mean for blocks. What was worse was that she was Irish. Even I thought she was pretty, and I didn't even like Irish girls. And I didn't like Jewish girls either; in fact, I didn't even realize I liked girls much at all until I was in college and saw some of those big Dutch girls, and some of those Swedish girls. I had a little crush on Linda Cuebas, nothing much, the daughter of my Puerto Rican super. She was just thirteen, and she was dark, and she had gray eyes. I nearly died when her family moved to Ho-ho-kus in Jersey. And I finally married a black girl, well, a mulatto girl, and I still love her, though she died in a horrible way a year after I graduated from law school, but I won't tell you about that now. See what was even worse was that it wasn't so bad she was an Irish girl, but she was Florry O'Neill, and all of us knew that at least up to that point she had been generally recognized to be the steady girlfriend of Jack Ryan, who was himself understood to have battled his way to be the warlord of the Fanwoods. Their leader. So Sugarman wasn't just escorting a pretty girl down the street, but he had taken trouble by the hand, which hand he was now holding after having taken a look at us and waved; trouble not just for himself, but for all the Bullets in the neighborhood. Florry turned her pretty face to us and smiled, and she waved too. To tell you the truth, no one in a million years would ever have expected such a thing to happen, because a girl takes a jacket not only because she likes a guy, but because she appreciates the shelter of being associated with the organization whose colors she puts on. No girl in her right mind would take off the Fanwoods' black and silver to put on our purple and gold. I mean, we just weren't fighters, not by nature. I was going to be a lawyer. We were doctors, dentists, pharmacists. We were going to college. That's why Grossman said, with a sigh that meant more than envy, "She must really love him." He knew she was in trouble, too.

"I think I'm gonna quit the Bullets," Dufner said.

Barney stuck his head out of his newspaper stand. "Is that that Irish girl little Freddy's with?"

"You got something against the Irish, Barney?" I asked.

"Schmuck, what do I got against? There are some very nice Irish. Mayor LaGuardia."

"He was a wop."

"Some of my best friends." Barney said. "But that kid is crazy."

"What do we know?" I said. "We don't know everything, Barney."

"I know crazy."

"She can go with whoever she likes. It's a free country. Sugarman knows what he's doing." I said that without conviction.

"A free country. Maybe for little Freddy right now. But he's gonna turn this place into a bomb shelter if you kids keep hanging out here. You kids ought to go home."

Zoo and Oserow and Grossman and Dufner had already started down the street. It was the first time Barney had ever expressed that he didn't want us to hang out. I couldn't say anything. I dribbled my basketball in front of his stand.

"I'll have to call the police," he said to himself, wistfully. "The police," shaking his head.

I dribbled the round ball all the way home.

We were just kids before we were the Bullets, and when we decided to get together and be the Bullets we didn't have anything big in mind. We didn't even have jackets in mind. We just figured we'd have a team, and practice, and play ball, schedule some games. We were always together anyway. It wasn't our intention to announce in any ostentatious way that we were something, the Bullets, put ourselves out as special around the park or the schoolyard. What you've got to understand about this neighborhood is that as soon as you say you're the Bullets it can be like a challenge for the Condors or the Fanwoods to use us to test their muscle, or just to kick our asses in general for the meanness of it or the territorial stupidity of it. Or maybe it would bring out the legendary Solomons to check us out. So at first we didn't try to let anyone know that we were the Bullets at all. We just wanted to be organized enough to play ball, have our own dances at the Y, and get the girls to come.

Now who were the Solomons? The Solomons were a dream. No one ever really understood who they were, but I remember sometimes, some really clear days in the neighborhood, little white clouds flew over the Palisades across the river, and the bridge hung in the blue sky like a silver hammock; I mean, it was like poetry in the air, and then someone would shout, "The Solomons. The Solomons are coming," and the streets would clear out because it was known that if the Solomons attacked it would be a slaughter. They were the atom bomb of gangs. Everyone talked about them, but no one ever saw them. They came from Solomon Avenue, but there was no Solomon Avenue in our neighborhood. There was one, way in the Bronx, but what gang would come to Washington Heights from the Bronx? There's a river to cross. I went to that Solomon Avenue once in the Bronx just out of curiosity. It was old people there at the time. No kids. No gang. There was no Solomon Avenue on any map of Manhattan. Maybe Solomon Avenue was someplace that existed in the minds of the Solomons, for the Solomons certainly existed in the minds of all the kids in the neighborhood. The story had it that they were perfect and thorough in their destruction of the gangs that opposed them. And there was a peculiar kind of justice associated with them, like they always picked on kids their own size. It was a mystery, but all you had to shout once was "The Solomons are coming," and stickball or slug or ring-o-leevio or marble season or whatever was being played on the streets, it would all be cleared out in a second, empty, everybody home.

So we were the Bullets anonymous until we met Baldeen.

No one had ever heard of someone called Baldeen before. No Baldeen in our neighborhood. That's what I mean about a neighborhood. Just when you think you know it, something new shows up. A Baldeen shows up. It was late August and we were practicing down by the river, and we noticed this guy watching us. He was older, maybe eighteen or so, and he squatted down and watched us, stroking his chin like he was thinking something over. Sugarman was our captain, and he talked to the guy because he recognized him. Baldeen actually lived in Sugarman's building. Sugarman never really knew him before, because who knows eighteen-year-olds? Baldeen said that he'd been watching the Bullets, and he was looking to manage a baseball team, and he wanted to manage the Bullets. "We don't need a manager, we're friends," Sugarman told him. But Baldeen picked up a bat and started to work with the infield on a pepper drill, and we'd never done it that way before, the ball coming at us so fast we didn't have time to think. I realized that was the trouble with our team—we were too many thinkers. And he gave us tips on positioning our feet and bending at the knees. We started learning things. Then he spread us out onto the diamond and started rapping these grounders at us, and we whipped the ball around the infield from Zoo at third to Sugarman at short to Jackobitz at second to me, Swanson, at first base. It felt so great. It felt like baseball. We felt like a team, like an infield for the first time. It made the Hudson River smell sweet. It made the George Washington Bridge hover like a dragonfly. Who was this Baldeen? Stamatakis belted fungos to the outfield, and we all were swinging like Ted Williams in batting practice. We finished with wind sprints around the field, which we had never done before, and ended up in a sweat, gathered around Baldeen at home plate. All of us had the same question. Who was this Baldeen? What was he doing with us kids? He was almost eighteen.

"You could have a good team," he said. His voice was real hoarse and weak, like he was missing half his throat. "What you need to do is practice a lot, and learn your fundamentals."

The word, "fundamentals," brought a little moan out of Stamatakis and Jackobitz.

"Baldeen wants to be our manager," said Sugarman.

"Why do you want to be our manager?" I asked.

He didn't answer. He just stared at me and then looked down at his feet. I was impressed.

"How old are you?" I asked.

Baldeen whispered into Sugarman's ear. Sugarman said, "He says he can get us into the Kiwanis League, and maybe into the American Legion League, so we can play at Babe Ruth Stadium." Babe Ruth Stadium was in the Bronx, right in the shadow of Yankee Stadium itself. It had a mowed grass outfield, and dirt infield without rocks, and a pitcher's mound. Playing there would be like riding around in a Lincoln Continental.

"We don't need leagues. We just want to play baseball," said Jackobitz.

"If you play hardball you play baseball," said Baldeen, himself, and he looked along the horizon as if he were watching a big bird fly along the Palisades toward Hoboken. I'd never heard anyone talk like that before, make you look for the meaning between the words. It was probably because he was older, I thought at first. All the kids were quiet. They were impressed, pondering the significance of "If you play hardball you play baseball." Then I thought maybe he was just stupid.

In my profession since, I've met a lot of stupid people who learned the trick of sounding smart.

Sugarman picked up a clod of dirt and crumbled it in his hand. "What Baldeen means is that if we get into the American Legion League or the Kiwanis, we get to play more games." He obviously wanted a manager.

"Games are baseball," Baldeen said.

"Boobs are baseball," said Stamatakis. He disliked Baldeen immediately. You could tell when Stamatakis was pissed because he would talk about breasts. Sometimes, if he was in a bad mood on the street, he would walk up to a woman, any woman, and say, "Tits, what time is it?" in a nasty way that would make me turn away as if I didn't know him. It was funny once, but then it got weird. I saw Stames with someone I thought was his mother once, a good looking blonde woman. Then Dinnerman told me that was his father who liked to dress up like a woman and wear a blonde wig. I don't know if that was true. You couldn't really trust Dinnerman, who I'll tell you a little more about later. Stamatakis never got to like Baldeen. We had to work on him every game to get him to play with the team. We'd never find us another long ball hitter like him. He was Babe Ruth—a fat kid with skinny legs and a threat to hit the ball over the fence every time he stepped up to the plate.

"Why does he want to be our manager? What does he get out of it?" Zoo asked Sugarman. Even though Baldeen was standing right there you didn't ask him anything usually, not directly. He had already taken Sugarman as his voice, as if he was a foreigner and needed a translator. All the time he managed us I never said more than one sentence to him directly. Sugarman looked at Baldeen after Zoo's question, and Baldeen picked up one of our old practice baseballs, one of those wrapped in electrician's tape to hold it together. It weighed a ton. He looked at it and chewed as if he was a pitcher with a jaw full of tobacco. I stared at him in amazement. I'd never seen anyone like Baldeen. He was acting something out, but who knew what it was? He stared at that old baseball as if he was reading something off it, then he leaned over and whispered in Sugarman's ear.

"First of all we need to get jackets. Bullet jackets," Sugarman said, smiling, pleased at the notion. Baldeen held the ball up under Zoo's nose, as if he wanted him to read off it too.

"Where do we get money for jackets?" Bernie Grossman asked. He was our catcher. He had just conned Mr. Grossman, the subway conductor, into investing in a mask, chest protector, and shinguards.

"We do a raffle," Sugarman said.

"Everyone does a raffle. We're sick of raffles." said Jackobitz.

"Then we'll need uniforms, spikes." Sugarman went on as Baldeen's voice.

"What do you think we are, millionaires?" Grossman asked.

"And it costs an entrance fee to get in the leagues, and we need baseballs, and we've got to pay to get in the ballpark."

"Where's your mother keep her money? You gonna pay for it? Between her tits?" Stamatakis banged his fist into the crook of his right elbow, giving Baldeen the sign.

"He still hasn't answered my question," Zoo said.

Baldeen whispered in Sugarman's ear. "We're gonna have to pay dues."

"Wait a second," Stamatakis' voice rose and dropped two octaves.

Dufner came in from the bushes by the railroad tracks

where he had hidden while we were doing the wind sprints. "What's going on?" he asked me.

"Baldeen wants to be our manager. He says we'll have to pay dues."

Dufner walked up and stood nose to nose with Baldeen, his sneakers overlapping Baldeen's shoes. "Jews pay dues. Shoes. Lose." He stepped away. "Baldeen the spaldeen. Cruise for a bruise." I never knew what was going on in Dufner's head, maybe nothing. He sure didn't show any respect for Baldeen's eighteen years. I almost liked that.

"We can get a sponsor," Jackobitz said.

"Who's gonna sponsor us?" Grossman shrugged.

"Your father," Dufner said. "We'll play on the A train."

"Maybe Barney'll sponsor us." Jackobitz looked at me. "You should ask him."

"Barney? Not if it costs him money," I said.

"Wait. We haven't even decided to have a manager. Who is this Baldeen? Now we have dues?" Stamatakis whined.

"I want you to say what you get out of it," Zoo said.

Baldeen was whispering to Sugarman. "He says he can get Nadelman to pitch for us. He's a lefty. With him and Schletzbaum we'll have two good pitchers. Bloustein will play for us too." He was a kid who was nothing but baseball, who wanted to try out for the majors as soon as he was old enough.

"Fuck this," said Stamatakis, and he turned his back on everyone and started up the path. The discussion was over. The rest of the Bullets followed Stamatakis.

Maybe it sounds like we weren't going to do it, but what I've learned is that if you're alive, and there's the next step to take, you take that step. That's probably what Sugarman did when Florry O'Neill put herself in front of him. He didn't think of

the greater good of the New York Bullets. He took her hand.
So even though we didn't like the idea of all that money we
decided to go ahead with it if we could. If you're fourteen and a
half you get a thrill out of the idea of jackets, leagues, uniforms, spikes. It makes you feel a little more powerful, something outside the influence of your parents. Baseball uniforms
are not practical, they're stupid clothes. They're baggy and
that's why they're great. You can only use them for baseball.
Jackets and uniforms would make us feel terrific like we had a
special purpose and the secret of victory.

What did Baldeen get out of it? No one ever figured it out.
You can't know everything. Maybe he got a little commission
off the jackets and uniforms, maybe a little rake off the dues.
Maybe he was an insecure eighteen-year-old guy who liked to
boss around a bunch of fifteen-year-olds. It was a big puzzle.

"I think he's a fruit," said Stamatakis. We were playing three
on three half court in the schoolyard. It was me, Stamatakis,
and Grossman against Dufner, Jackobitz's little brother, Hubby, and Dinnerman, whom I mentioned before.

"A fruit?" Dinnerman said, and he threw up one of his
weird hookshots, that he would take from anywhere on the
court without looking at the basket. A lot of times it went in.
He was in all ways a gunner.

"What does that mean, a fruit?" Grossman asked.

Stamatakis grabbed the rebound and passed it out to me. He
never jumped for a rebound, but took up so much space under
the basket that no one usually could get close enough to take it
away from him. Bob Cousy was my idol. I liked to drive to the
basket, dribble between my legs, behind my back, and go. I
liked to beat my man, get around him, who in this case was
Dufner, so it was not too difficult. Dufner had potential, but

all he liked to do was foul. You couldn't wear a belt when you played with him because he'd grab it when you went up in the air, or try to trip you as you went by, or put an elbow in your ribs. I faked him left and got around him and went up with the ball, and I loved that feeling of flying to the basket, then pulling your legs up so you get another kick, floating a second and laying the ball in. I bounced off Stamatakis, who was still there under the basket, and the ball spun around the rim and in. Two points.

"What do you mean, a fruit?" Grossman asked again.

"Does he look at you as if he wants to suck all the time?" Dinnerman asked. "Does his mouth always have that pucker?" Dinnerman knew a lot about queers. He was older than us and a lot bigger. He lived with his mother, who didn't work, and he had to support her. He did that by going down to Times Square and rolling queers. He was the toughest Jewish guy in the neighborhood. His responsibilities made him tough. Though he wasn't stupid, they kept leaving him back because he didn't have time for school. In his heart he was really a nice guy, even though he was a delinquent, actually a criminal. We respected him, and would have liked him to be on the Bullets, because his reputation in the neighborhood would be a little protection, but there was no chance he'd ever put on a purple and gold jacket, even though he came around the schoolyard a lot to play basketball with us and he gunned his hooks. All he liked to do was shoot. He wouldn't pass off. He wouldn't guard his man. He'd never hustle; not playing basketball. He relaxed at basketball.

"He's not a fruit," I said.

"He wants to hang out with us kids. He's a fruit," Stamatakis insisted. "He's eighteen. Maybe older."

"I'm almost eighteen. Does that make me a fruit?" Dinner-man asked.

"What do you mean, a fruit?" Grossman was a little behind.

"It takes one to know one," Stamatakis said to Dinnerman, a dangerous move, but the gunner only laughed.

"A fruit likes boys instead of girls," I whispered to Grossman. "Ohhhh."

"We should ask Sugarman," Dufner said. "Sugarman the boogerman. Baldeen is always breathing in his ear."

"Come on. Sugarman likes girls," I said.

"You never know who likes what," said Dinnerman in his wisdom. "I met this queer once who was with a model. She was gorgeous."

"I'm gonna quit the Bullets," said Dufner.

"You already ordered your jacket," I reminded him. "You paid your deposit."

Dufner passed in bounds to Hubby, who dribbled past Grossman into the corner. Hubby was just thirteen, an intense little athlete, who ended up beating out his brother at second base, from which disappointment Vernon never re-covered. I tried to switch and pick up Hubby but Dufner had me by the shirt. Hubby heaved up a one-hander and it bounced around the rim.

"Ass. Ass. Ass." Dufner used body english to get the ball down. It went in. "Assed it in, that's twenty. We win."

"That's just sixteen," said Grossman. "How do you get twenty?"

"Your sister's sixteen and sucks my pickle," said Dufner.

"One more word about my sister," Grossman warned him.

"And what?" Dufner said.

"You guys have got sixteen," Grossman said.

"Why don't we play to thirty?" Dinnerman said.

"Your sister's a fruit," said Dufner.

"Dufner...."

"What's wrong? I said your sister likes boys. What's wrong with that? She likes girls?"

"Play the game," said Hubby. "It's gonna get dark."

"Okay. Sixteen to twelve." said Stamatakis. "We go to thirty, and you guys are fruits."

"Kiss my knuckle," said Dinnerman, which I always remembered, though I didn't get it till years later.

The baseball season was almost over, and the marble season was upon us. Florry O'Neill had solved the question of whether Sugarman liked girls or Baldeen, but her simple act of slipping into someone's Bullet jacket raised many other questions. Was Jack Ryan pissed? Would Sugarman have to face him down alone like in *High Noon*? Would the Bullets have to rumble with the Fanwoods? We were not rumblers in any sense; in fact, none of us had ever rumbled. Who knew anything about what would happen in this neighborhood? Every minute each of us had an eye out for the Fanwoods coming round the corner. It was like expecting an invasion, like the citizens of Paris waiting for the inevitable Nazis.

Though we didn't know it then, this was to be the last marble season. I don't know if other neighborhoods had these marble seasons, but during and right after the Second World War we had one each fall on 173rd Street. Marbles, immies, peewees, boulders, purees—they were the medium of exchange for about two weeks every autumn on my street, as important as the twenty-four dollars worth of trinkets and beads that originally bought Manhattan Island. The Bullets were almost too old for marble season, but we did it anyway because it was something to do. It was a little festival. Kids rigged up cigar boxes, or other kinds of sturdy boxes, with holes just a little bigger than marbles, and they'd set these boxes up against the curb, and from across the street kids would gamble their precious marbles, shoot them towards the holes in hopes of winning five or ten or fifteen for one, according to the size of the hole and the distance from the box. The whole of the north side of the hill from Broadway to Fort Washington was little entrepreneurs lined up with their cigar-box establishments, and the other side was a flow of young gamblers. It was busy, up and down the street. But then no one owned cars yet. By the next year cars were parked bumper to bumper, and there was no room for a marble season. This year Dufner showed up with a box.

"You're almost fifteen, Dufner," I said.

"Lean, mean, and fifteen," he said. "And I've got luck." He held a prize up in front of my face.

"Let me see that," I took it from his hand. This was a peewee puree of inestimable beauty. A puree is a transparent marble of uniform color, and peewee is obvious. This one was deep red, like a ruby, like a drop of blood. A kid falls in love with such a puree. Dufner showed it around before he set up his box. Everyone wanted it. You could see the thrill when they looked at it. It was a marble they had always dreamed about. They lined up to shoot at his box. Kids came from everywhere, their pockets heavy with marbles. It felt like wealth to walk out of your house on marble season with a big bag of marbles in your pocket. Nothing has come along to replace that feeling.

"Here it is, suckers." He let the kids admire the precious red drop. "Just get it in the hole." The hole he made just big enough to force a marble through, but it would never admit one shot from across the street. Other boxes got some business, but Dufner's was the star. Even though he made it impossible, and everyone knew it, he ended up the biggest marble millionaire on the block. He knew how to exploit the beauty of one peewee puree. And he kept his little treasure as well. It was like a lesson in America. On the last day of the season Dufner stood at the top of the hill on Broadway and 173rd Street with an expression of triumph on his face. Over what? Over marble season? Over childhood? And he let all the immies and boulders and marbles and peewees go. He scattered them down the hill, dumped them from his bags like they were nothing but mothballs, while all the kids scrambled for them.

"What about your peewee puree?" I asked him. "Let me see it again." You see I figured that he figured that with such a peewee puree he didn't need the other marbles, he could always become rich, like someone with power to predict the horses.

"I let it go," he said.

"What for? You're crazy," I said. I asked everyone, and I looked up and down the curb. No one had picked it up. I went back to Dufner whose smile made me feel two years old.

"Nobody's got it," I said.

"Probably went down the sewer," he said.

"Your little peewee?" I could feel my voice crack and rise up. Something seemed horrible.

"My little peewee. I threw it in the sewer."

Nothing was precious to Dufner. He wouldn't say any more

about it. He was another guy in the neighborhood you don't figure out. He didn't respect anything, or maybe he knew that this was the end of all the marble seasons.

Baldeen called a few practices in late September, even though for us the baseball season was over. It was almost World Series time. The Yankees were in it again, and the Brooklyn Dodgers, a subway series. That was the year of Bill Bevens, Cookie Lavagetto, and of course Al Gionfriddo's robbing Joe DiMaggio of a home run. It seemed a shame to me they were both Italian. The last practice was one warm Sunday in October. Baldeen wanted us to practice bunting. He was a fanatic about it. He wanted infield drill too, because by next spring most of us would be over fifteen, and he wanted us in the American Legion League, and a sharp fearless infield made a great impression. Standing in the batter's box wasn't easy for me in the first place. To wait while someone threw a hard ball in your direction, some kid who didn't have much control over it in the first place, was not something I did naturally. To bunt, I mean to square away and face the pitcher with your whole body, that was counter to my sense of self-preservation. My big problem at the bat was that I stepped into the bucket; that is, I batted right-handed, and when the pitcher came down with his delivery my left foot jumped out of the batter's box. That was fear.

"Tell him to stand in there," Baldeen shouted to Sugarman at short.

"Stand in there, Swanny," Sugarman shouted at me.

I tried. I concentrated. I watched Schletzbaum wind up. He was fast, and he could even throw a curve. But he was wild, and I knew that, and I was prepared for the worst pitch, which was a fast ball at my head, and as much as I tried to hold it there my leg moved by itself out of the batter's box as soon as Schletzbaum let go of the ball.

"Stand in there," Baldeen, exasperated, shouted at me all by himself.

"Mel Ott moves his leg," I shouted back.

"You're not Ott," said Baldeen.

"So does Stan Musial."

"Stan Musial hits the ball," someone shouted, and before I could think Schletzbaum had wound up and the pitch came in before I knew it, and I swung at it, and I connected for a line drive over second base. A solid shot. I'll never forget how good that felt, connected from the earth under my feet, up my legs, turned by my waist and hips, up my spine, through my arms, into my wrists and hands on the bat. Smash. I was one piece, moving into the ball. Thick as the Palisades. Fluid as the big Hudson River.

"Attaboy, Swanny. That's the way to hit the ball. It's easy if you don't step in the bucket," Sugarman shouted. Baldeen looked unimpressed. He signaled for me to bunt a few. I always thought that was a bad piece of coaching at that point, and I would never do that if I ever became a coach. He should have let me hit a few more at that point, consolidate my confidence.

As soon as I squared away, held the bat loosely in front of myself, watched that pellet being shot at me from Schletzbaum's cannon, all my fear suddenly came back. As far as I could see only crazy people did that. I'll tell you I loved the idea of baseball, and once we got our uniforms I loved being on the Bullet's baseball team. All of us jumping on the subway dressed in the profound purposes of baseball was very great in my life, riding together to a game in Van Cortland Park; but to have to square away while someone threw a rock at your body, that I did not like at all.

Baseball season was over anyway, and most of us were thinking basketball, and we were thinking of sponsoring our first dance. You could sponsor a game and dance at the Y if you were registered there as an official club and played in one of the Y basketball leagues. If you really wanted to do it right you hired a band, and you played a game beforehand, and invited all the girls you ever knew for free, and charged the guys half a buck to get in. The money was supposed to go for buying basketball uniforms, but usually you could barely pay the band.

"We'll have Deuce Douros and the Aces," said Sugarman.

"No," said Dufner. "That's bullshit. I'd rather have Guy Lombardo records."

"What do you mean? They play mambo, they play cha-cha. They play rock and roll."

"Yeah, they play it," said Dufner. "And always they lose."

"How about Shep Fields and his Rippling Rhythm," someone said.

"Better than Douche Douros and his Pussies," Dufner said.

"They've even got a singer," Sugarman insisted.

"Who? Sylvia Tweet? She sings like Elmer Fudd getting seasick."

"What do you want? Patti Page?"

"'How much is that doggy in the window?'" Dufner said.

"Douros is cheap."

"Yuk."

"He's got his own drums. It'll be a great dance. The girls'll come. They'll even come from the Bronx."

Deuce was almost a Bullet, but he didn't like sports. We

went to school together. He liked photography, and he played the drums. When he wasn't working at his father's restaurant he was practicing. He was fanatical about the drums but unfortunately had no sense of rhythm. Once he made a pilgrimage to Queens, where Buddy Rich lived, to see if he could get the man he thought was the greatest technical drummer in the whole world to be his teacher. He had, Deuce told me, complete independence of all four limbs—could play one rhythm with his right hand, another with his left, and two more with each of his feet. Deuce Douros wanted that. I had heard Buddy Rich, but I preferred Max Roach or Art Blakey, both of whom had "ideas," or even Denzel Best who played with George Shearing, brushes so tasteful. Max particularly. He knew how to use silence. Anyway Deuce went to Buddy Rich's house and he rang the bell. He could hear the great drummer practicing. He rang the bell again, and knocked on the door. No answer. He walked around and knocked on all the windows. Paradiddles endlessly flowing from that house, but no one answered. Deuce stayed there and listened, occasionally knocking. Buddy Rich never answered the door, but Deuce was satisfied. He returned to Washington Heights inspired.

I hung out sometimes on weekends with Deuce and with another friend of his, Bruce Kcock. The kid's name was actually Kcock. He liked the name; in fact, he bought a Bullet jacket even though he never played for us, and he didn't embroider Bruce on the jacket but put his last name. Once Mr. Kutzer, a gym teacher who didn't know him, saw him with the jacket on and took him to the principal's office. Maybe his name was why he never got married. Who would want to be Mrs. Kcock? He loved to gamble, and that was why he never went to gym. He was always shooting craps in some corner. He had his own roulette table at home, and on the weekends he always knew where there was a poker game. Both his mother and his grandmother gave him big allowances, so he'd have at least twenty dollars every Saturday night that he'd blow in a poker game with some guys in their twenties down on 167th Street. They let him play. They took his money. Deuce and I would walk him to his game, then go to a movie or whatever, and check on him afterwards. If he was busted by then we'd all go back to Deuce's dad's restaurant and raid the freezer and eat all the biscuit tortoni and spumoni. Now I think Kcock is a dealer in Vegas; in fact, I think he's a supervisor.

"Deuce Douros and the Aces is the best idea," I said. "Who else are we going to get?"

"That's what I say," Sugarman said.

"Why not The Empathetics?" Dufner said. "I was at a dance with them on 166th Street last week, and they were great. All of them sing."

"They're union, Dufner. We can't pay union scale," said Sugarman.

"Cha-cha-cha," said Dufner. "Let's get Tito Puente."

"Schmuck."

"C'mon. Play basketball," said Hubby, reminding us why we were all in the schoolyard in the first place.

"Shit. There's Ginzy," said Grossman. The rule was that if you called "next" and waited through the whole game you got to play the winners. Ginzy was hanging out under the basket waiting to call "next." He always wore the same spotted black pants and a white shirt stained with a week's meals. His father owned the funeral parlor on 174th Street and Broadway and to earn his allowance Ginzy had to sleep with the corpses on weekends, the watchman's night off. When he sweated he smelled like formaldehyde. His face was a dead face without color, black hair pasted down like a coffin lid, eyes always bloodshot from lying awake with the corpses. He dragged his body around as if at the slightest provocation he was ready to join those he slept with.

Ginzy was there, and as soon as we got to the basket he called, "next." I threw up a shot. Swish.

"Hey, Ginzy, any pretty girls on the slabs?" Dufner went after him. "You ever sniff dead pussy?"

"I was here. I got next," Ginzy said. He was impervious to insult. That's the definition of a creep. You had to like him; at least you had to like the idea of Ginzy the Creep.

You couldn't figure out why he wanted to play basketball. He never moved, or if he did he fell down. If you threw him the ball he'd generally lose it out of bounds. As soon as the game started he got so excited he'd start to sweat and drool, and his eyes would tear so he could hardly see. Poor Ginzy. He smelled so strong no one would guard him. If he had any kind of shot at all he'd be a real scoring threat. We had ten guys including Ginzy so we decided to play full court. I scored three straight baskets, using Stamatakis for a pick, then Dufner tripped me and Stamatakis both so that Stames fell on top of me. You ever find yourself under a hippo? It slowed me down a little. Me and Stames were ready to go after him the next time he got the ball in bounds, but Dufner had a sixth sense. As soon as he got the ball he called "time," because he got one of his mysterious nosebleeds, and I was nowhere near him at that moment. He often got these nosebleeds, especially when he ran, or he could get them at will, especially when he knew someone was angry enough to punch his face. He was smart.

He knew it was easier on him to bleed himself than to have someone he's pissed off do it for him. His nose punched itself out, so to speak.

We kept playing while Dufner held his head back and pressed his handkerchief against his nose. I stole the ball from Mamoulian on his dribble and tossed it down court to Ginzy who caught it for once. He stood there holding it against his stomach. "Ginzy. Ginzy," I shouted as I followed the ball down court, but he just held it. I went right up to him and tried to take the ball out of his belly, but he spun around and ran with it, without even dribbling. "I'm on your team," I said, but Ginzy trusted no team. He ran to the basket, and as if he were tossing a shot-put he threw the ball up in the air and it went in. "Two points," Ginzy shouted. He had scored like that once before, and we argued a little about it, but then we gave him his two points because for Ginzy the game was a different game. There was no argument this time. We all looked at Dufner.

Dufner was waving his bloody handkerchief, gesturing frantically at the fence. The schoolyard was enclosed on the 173rd and the 174th street sides by a wire mesh storm fence twelve feet high. At first all I saw was a blur along this fence, but then I began to sort it out. This was Fanwoods in their black and silver jackets. They lined the fences on both streets. They stood with their fingers gripping the fence. Some of them were wearing black gloves. Most of them were wearing shades. I had to hold myself real tight because otherwise I would have shit right there in my pants in the schoolyard. The worst thing was, they didn't make a sound.

"Oh Jesus," Mamoulian said.

"Jesus is on their side," Dufner said. Nothing fazed him.

That was a virtue. "I quit the Bullets yesterday, remember?"

Mamoulian was starting to cry. "I told my mother I'd be back by three." I put my hand on his shoulder.

"You should have had your mother write you a note," Dufner said. "Look why don't you write a note, and I'll forge your mother's signature."

"Dufner," I said. That was enough. I couldn't figure out if he was scared. Maybe he was, but it didn't show. Sugarman stood by himself, looking at one fence, and then the other. "Sugarman," I said. "You know those guys?"

He looked at me, and then away, and didn't say anything. There was no escape. Everything was so quiet. The Fanwoods had never come to our schoolyard before, except sometimes individually, but never in a war party. It felt like a movie—the Apaches on all the ridges surrounding the covered wagons. I felt separate from the time there, like what was going to happen wasn't my life, like the dark Fanwoods at the fence were shimmering off into a void of other places, not here, with me. I bounced my basketball just to feel it come up from the ground.

Ginzy was running around like a dog. I don't know what he was doing. He stumbled past the Fanwoods at the fence shouting "Two points. Two points." To the Fanwoods we were all creeps. I knew that. But poor Ginzy wasn't even a Bullet. He didn't even know that these were Fanwoods.

"You see," Grossman said to Sugarman. "See what happens?"

"Shut up," said Sugarman.

"You get us all killed, just for a girlfriend."

"No one gets killed. We just stick together." Sugarman acted like he felt obliged to be our leader, but his voice sounded like the squeak of a door.

"I don't want to miss dinner," Mamoulian was crying and grinning.

As far as what I was feeling, we were all killed already. I mean, if cowards die a thousand times, I was breaking the record. I never liked to fight. I never even liked to clench my fist. Maybe that's why I became a lawyer. I'd let them fight. But most of the Bullets were that way, and that was why we were the Bullets, together, chicken smarts. I died more than once for each of the Fanwoods standing by the fence, two or three times for each of the black gloves on their hands, for their dark jackets, their narrow eyes, for their cool and their silence as they surrounded us.

"Let 'em come," said Hubby Jackobitz.

He was a year younger than most of us, and he wasn't afraid of anything. I watched him get into a fight once with two fifteen-year-old kids, and they were sorry they started it. He knocked one guy down by smashing up on his chin with his skull, and then he bit off a piece of his ear. Then he went for the other kid, who was by then scared out of his wits, and he was grinding for his neck with his teeth when his brother, Vernon, showed up and pulled him off. That kid was never going to college. He was too cranky. He ended up in Israel, fighting the wars.

"Come on in. Come on," he shouted.

"Shut up, Hubby," said Mamoulian.

"Fanwoods are faggots," said Hubby.

"You should talk to them. You should talk to Jack Ryan," I told Sugarman.

"Wh. . .why should I talk to them?"

"She's wearing your jacket. That's why they're here."

"It's a free country. She didn't have to take my jacket."

"You didn't have to give it to her either. That's why we're in trouble."

The Fanwoods started to move. I felt myself stiffen, like my shoulders rose up around my neck. The air around me broke up into yellow canaries pulling me apart in a twittering of sound. This moment was not real, I thought to myself. They entered the schoolyard slowly, as if they were shy, one at a time; but they were casual, slowly closing on us nine Bullets and Ginzy. They were smiling. "You've got to say next if you want the next game," Ginzy said.

"Next. Next. Next. Next. Next," the Fanwoods said, one at a time.

"Okay. You guys have got the next game," Ginzy said.

"Go home, Ginzy," Sugarman said.

"We're playing till thirty."

"Go home."

Ginzy's white face got whiter. He wiped his shirtsleeve across the drool on his mouth. He looked around as if for the first time he understood what was going on. His head drooped foward on his neck as if it had suddenly gotten heavier. He started towards the gate past the Fanwoods. One of them made a move towards him, but then smelled the formaldehyde and stepped back. Ginzy was pitiful, but at that moment powerful too. I envied him, wished I was disgusting. It's the power of a cockroach, a slug, a skunk. It's the anticharisma. It's being the something else that no one wants to touch.

"Which one of them is Ryan?" Stamatakis asked me, looking at the five Fanwoods who hadn't come down into the school-yard. We figured one of them was Ryan, and the rest were his lieutenants. They looked so casual there, leaning against a car, joking as if there wasn't violence just about to happen. I caught the eyes of one of them and for an instant looked into them as if through a telescope. He was small as my father. And it was as if he drew all the fear out of me. I was suddenly okay. I could easily have been a Fanwood myself, if we lived on the east side of Broadway, if I enjoyed to fight.

"You should go up there and talk to Ryan yourself," Stames told Sugarman. "At least you should talk to him."

"Yeah, talk to him," Sugarman said. "Florry told me he would kill me, probably kill her too."

"Was Florry sorry?" Dufner grinned. How did he do it?

"You're a jerk," Sugarman said.

"Jerk me off," said Dufner. He threw his head back and shouted out of nowhere. "The Bullets eat green hu-er snot. The Bullets are purple faggots."

The Fanwoods closed in on us so slowly you almost couldn't feel it. Whoever Ryan was, he and his lieutenants watched us like some field commanders. The littlest kid, their mascot— maybe he was nine years old—walked up to Stamatakis, who was the biggest of us all by far.

"Hey. You're a big guy," he said. He wound up and threw a punch into Stames' solar plexus. I mean the kid was less than half Stames' size. Stames grabbed the kid's fist, but let go as he remembered the thirty or so Fanwoods surrounding the nine of us. That was the way they did it, a kind of ritual, a protocol for violence. They send one of their little brothers to pick on the biggest guy, and when the guy gets mad, and even pushes the kid back a little, doesn't even hurt him, then the Fanwoods move in, bring their power down on him, destroy him, bust all his bones. Stamatakis looked so weird and unhappy, so help-less, this little tiny kid pushing him across the schoolyard.

"You're a fat faggot," the kid said. He was just a little buck-toothed, red-headed Irish kid who probably didn't know what a faggot was. The commanders were so cool at the fence, watching their men move around us like big cats. A certain spectator inside me was fascinated, but the rest of me was scared. I felt as if my real body wasn't there. Like this was a nightmare. Like my flesh and blood wasn't doing this, and all that was here hovering in the scene was a witness, no flesh and blood. Wishful thinking. I was scared shitless. Then one of the Fanwoods grabbed my basketball, and I was right there. This kid grabbed it and threw it to another Fanwood. They tossed it back and forth, didn't even dribble. Didn't even go to the basket. They didn't look like they could go to the basket. It was obvious these Irish kids couldn't even play basketball. They could fight, and that was it. Where was the satisfaction in that? Even at that moment I felt a little sorry for them.

Dufner approached one of the Fanwoods. "All the Bullets are fruits. They're all faggots." This Fanwood drove one of his black gloves like a stroke of light into Dufner's gut, and that made me feel almost good; I mean, he was a traitor at that moment. He collapsed to the ground, and his nosebleed started up again. They were still tossing my basketball around. I watched that little buck-toothed kid push poor Stamatakis across the schoolyard. He had eight other Fanwoods behind him.

"Hey, Bullet? You want your basketball back?" One of them held it out to me as if he was going to give it back.

"If you could play basketball, you wouldn't have to fight," I said like a jerk. He smashed the ball into my face, though I luckily bent my head, and it caught mostly my forehead. It could have changed the shape of my nose. I deserved it. One of them picked it up and tossed it, and I jumped and deflected it off my hand, then stopped. I could have intercepted at almost any point but thought it better they throw the ball around rather than my body.

"Sugarman," I said. I don't know why. I could see them pounding Stamatakis now against the wall. "Sugarman. Sugarman." He turned away from me so they wouldn't know that he was Sugarman.

"You want the ball back now, Bullet? Here." He pounded the ball into my gut, then pulled his knife out of it, and it deflated in my arms. I couldn't believe it. My arms trembled as it lost its shape. That was my ball. That was two weeks' work delivering prescriptions after school for Ray Drugs. "You bastards," I breathed with the air escaping from my ball. "Mick Pricks. Irish sons of bitches." If my father had heard me maybe he would have put the knife in my belly. I couldn't see anything, my eyes full of tears. I think the fighting must have started because I heard a lot of grunts and shouts around me, and my flattened ball fell to the ground and I started swinging wildly at all the air around me as if I could beat the whole schoolyard atmosphere clean of Fanwoods. I couldn't hear the high-pitched whistle, and didn't see the Fanwoods run for the exits, and was still fighting everything when Stamatakis grabbed me and held me. "Take it easy, Swanny."

The Fanwoods were disappearing down the street, and a few seconds later a squad car crawled into view, and a couple of cops walked down by the fence, looked in at us—only Bullets left—and walked on. Schletzbaum, who lived in an apartment right across the street from the schoolyard, had looked out his window, seen what was going on, and had called his father at the precinct house.

Stamatakis let go of me. I'd never felt like this before. I'd never felt my Irish up before. If I'd touched one of them he would have been dead. I wouldn't have stopped. I would have killed him. I didn't like that feeling. It was like looking down into the smell of a sewer and not seeing the bottom.

Mamoulian brought my sad basketball and put it in my hands. I looked at it. So what? For this I went nuts? For this I could hurt someone?

"You can patch it. Get a bike patch kit at Strauss, like an innertube patch," said Mamoulian. I stuck my finger in the gash in the ball.

"Next time we'll have all our guys here, and we'll jump them when they show up," Hubby said.

"I don't think so," I said.

"Why did I become a Bullet?" Dufner said.

"I'm an Armenian," said Mamoulian, for no reason.

"I'm not afraid of the Fanwoods. I'm not chicken," said Hubby.

"I know you're not," I said. "But that doesn't mean we're going to fight. There are other ways to settle. If you want to fight, why don't you join them? Join the Fanwoods."

"I'm a kike mick greaseball wop," Dufner said.

"I don't want to join them," said Hubby. "I'm a New York Bullet."

I went over to Sugarman, who was rolling some pebbles around with the toe of his sneaker, not looking at anyone.

"Sugarman," I said. "You're the captain here, right?"

He looked at me as if it was none of my business. Sugarman had deep emotions. He didn't like to let anyone get inside them. "What is that supposed to mean?" he said.

"If she wasn't wearing your jacket this wouldn't have happened, right? Things were going all right before."

"So."

"I mean don't you feel like you ought to do something, as the Bullet captain, as Florry O'Neill's boyfriend."

"You want me to pay for your basketball?" he asked, but he knew that's not what I wanted.

"No."

"What?"

"You should go talk to Ryan. Talk to him."

A Baby Ruth wrapper rode in on a gust of wind. He took a few steps away from me and picked it up. "Why should *I* talk to him?"

"It could help."

Sugarman carefully folded the Baby Ruth wrapper. "I'll talk to Baldeen."

"Baldeen? What's he got to do with this?"

"Baldeen can go talk to them."

"Jesus, Sugarman," I said. I didn't know what else to say. You can't push anyone to make him other than himself. He put the Baby Ruth wrapper in his pocket, glanced in my eyes real quick, and walked away.

"I hope she clamps up on you," I said after him, though I don't think he heard me, and I'm glad, because it was a stupid thing to say. "Somebody walk with him to 178th Street," I said. "We better leave together." Stames caught up with Sugarman.

"Funny," I said, walking with Zoo towards my house.

"What's funny?" he asked. He got hit in the face once and was swelling up under his eye.

"I don't know," I said. "I don't feel too bad. I feel pretty good." That was true. My ex-basketball was crumpled in my hands. I knew that Sugarman was never going to talk to Jack

Ryan; that if anyone was going to do it, I was the one. That didn't even scare me.

"Look at your eye," I said.

Zoo started to laugh. "It looks like a weird poached egg," I said.

"Didn't even hurt," he said.

"It hurt me more when they stabbed my basketball," I said. We both laughed.

"What a bunch of assholes," said Zoo.

That's right, I thought. That's it. After all, I could talk to him. Jack Ryan was just a person.

I walked past my mother, tossed my flattened ball onto the couch, and closed the door of my room behind me. I heard her come up and stand by my door. She knocked lightly.

"What?"

"You left without breakfast. You don't look like you had a thing to eat all day."

"I had breakfast."

"What? A little bowl of Cheerios? You didn't even put in a banana. What kind of food value does that have if you play ball all day?"

"I wasn't hungry."

"What happened to your basketball?"

"I'll fix it. I'll put a patch on it."

"You think money grows on trees. You spend all day playing ball. I've got to clean the house. Your father's coming home tomorrow."

"Mom!" I just couldn't stand it when she bugged me like that. I'd rather she'd just tell me what to do.

"The floors are still dirty."

"I'll clean them."

"At least take the garbage down."

Finally. Instructions. What a relief. Does every mother of a teenage kid antagonize him like that? Mine drove me nuts. I mean, a mother has all the power, and she can be perfectly straight with it, but she exerts it by devious means. She has to make you feel guilty, so you won't forget her for the rest of your life. I was in my thirties before I could ever love her again, before I could stop smirking every time I thought of the *Horn and Hardart Children's Hour* song on the radio—"Less work for mother"—before I could stop thinking of her as a subversive agent for the enemy—"Just lend her a hand."

I went down to the courtyard with two bags of garbage in my arms. Our courtyard was across the street from Jayhood Wright Park. This was a small park, about four blocks square, that looked like a little patch of Central Park. Along the south wall there once had been a line of poplar trees that a hurricane took down in 1943. I used to see those trees out of my bedroom window, and I loved them. You could see the George Washington Bridge behind them. They were tall, and slim, and elegant. And the bridge behind them was powerful. Its long arc moved you like a steel whip. The trees were gone, and they were never replanted, but I could dream them back into place. They made me think America, how I loved America. I don't know why. It was a feeling in my heart when I was fourteen, still proud of it after the Second World War, not yet aware of how terrifying our new adventure in Korea was becoming. It was a pure dream in the absence of trees. Sea to shining sea—an image that is tarnished now for this Irish-Jewish lawyer by the years since of bittersweet history. O yeah, God bless America, I love it for its people in the sixties, for the clowns and their causes. And it makes me crazy, and I despise it, to think of the relentless deceit and inhumanity of our leaders in the Vietnam War, in Chile, in Central America. So I stood there with garbage in my arms and daydreamed into the space of trees the big wind had cleared, and stared at my bridge, when suddenly three Fanwoods appeared in the court-yard entrance, their black and silver jackets. A shock, a thrill went up my spine. I was glad I wasn't wearing my Bullet jacket.

One of them was that little red-headed mascot with buck-teeth and freckles, and another looked like the kid who had stabbed my basketball, though I wasn't absolutely sure I remembered what he looked like. This was one of those puffy-faced little Irish kids who already looked like too much beer and Canadian Club. The third was a wiry nervous-looking kid, who looked like I sometimes imagined I looked myself. He seemed to have thoughts. I liked to look at him. The other two grinned when they saw me, as if they had been hungry and finally found something to eat. The little kid approached me. I knew that act real well now, but this time he was carrying a big kitchen knife that his mother was probably looking for right at that moment. To slice the potatoes.

"You a Jew?" It was the first time that question had ever hit me. I mean it. All its centuries of stupidity, meanness, irration-ality, focused on me through this little Huck Finn of a kid with a butcher knife in his hand. I mean six and one half million or more of my mother's people had died in the Holocaust because of the same madness that had a nine-year-old kid shaking a knife in my face. "I said are you a Jew?" In my heart, I mean deep in my heart, I didn't understand what he was asking. The slim guy came over and took the knife away from the little one. "Leave him alone," he said.

The pudgy kid pushed in front and shoved me in the chest. "He said are you a Jew?" You can't write that word down the way he pronounced it, as if it was the lowest of the curses.

"No," I said, which was half true. My mother always told me to deny it.

Antisemitism, she told me, you couldn't argue with it. It made no sense, and never would, and it would always be there. It was hard to be a Jew. Or half a Jew. She had lost a whole small village full of relatives in Buchenwald and Belsen. I don't know why I didn't just drop the garbage in front of them and run.

"Okay, then what nationality are you?" the little kid asked.

"I'm American," I said.

The kid squinted in puzzlement and looked at his bigger companions. The pudgy one shoved me in the chest again. "You're a wiseass kid. I think you're a Jew. He asked you what nationality you are."

"I'm a Unitarian," I said. I figured that was a safe one.

"What's a Unit...a Unit....What does that mean?"

"You're not a Jew?" said Chubby.

"I said I'm a Unitarian."

For some reason the little kid was starting to laugh. I had suddenly become a comedian for him.

"Okay," said the chubby one, his hands on his hips. "You say you're not a Jew, let's hear the catechism."

I shook my head. This kid was really stupid. I looked at the skinny one. His expression never changed.

"Say the catechism," said Chubby. "I want to hit him. Give me that knife. I want to cut him."

"Leave him alone," said the thin one. "He looks like he's going to cry. I don't like to see a kid cry."

I didn't feel like I was going to cry. Maybe he saw the wind in my eyes. That always makes them tear.

"If he's not a Jew, make him say the catechism."

"A Unitarian doesn't say the catechism," said the thin one.

"What does he say?"

The little kid was laughing, bending over, jumping in the air, saying "Unitarian. Unitarian. Unitarian." I don't know what he found so funny. I wouldn't be surprised if later in his life he became one.

"You're a wiseass," Chubby said to me, but I could feel the danger had passed. More or less I had talked my way out of it.

"Leave him alone. Let's go."

"Fuck," said Chubby, and he knocked the garbage out of my arms, and he and the little one kicked it all over the courtyard. That was when I made a strategic mistake. I was standing there next to the skinny one watching them kick my garbage around, and I said to him, "Do you know Jack Ryan?"

"Are you joking with me, punk?" he said. That was the last thing I heard. He must have hit me with something, probably his fist. Next thing I was lying in the middle of the garbage, the kids were gone, and Mr. Cuebas, our Puerto Rican super, was pushing at my shoulder with his foot.

"Whon hoppen to you?" he asked.

"I fell down," I said.

"I going tell you mama."

"What will you tell her?"

"I spend three hours, make this courtyard clean, and you come put shit on it like this."

"Tell her that."

"Puerco. Puercos delincuentes."

"I'm sorry, Mr. Cuebas. I'll pick it all up."

"I doan unnastan whon hoppen here."

"Your daughter is very pretty, Mr. Cuebas."

"Your daughter very pretty, Mr. Cuebas."

He never trusted me. A year later, when I started to go out with his daughter a little, we had to meet around the corner. I always thought their move to Ho-ho-kus could have been partly to get her away from me.

As soon as my father got home the next evening he asked me where I'd got my black eye. I hadn't even looked in the mirror, but my mother had seen it and had wanted to take me to the hospital. I wouldn't go. It was a great one, blue underneath, hemorrhaged bright red in the white.

"I don't know," I said.

"What does the other bum look like?"

"I didn't see him."

"You can't say that. You have to see him, otherwise what's the satisfaction in it?" He pointed at the scar on his cheek. "See this?" I often stared at that scar when we were watching *Milton Berle* or *The Show of Shows*. It was like a pale blue eye half shut that ran from his cheekbone to just above his lip. "I know damn well where I got this." And he told me the story for the thousandth time of his fight with Sean Rattigan on whose land his family and their little band of tinkers were camped when he was only sixteen. Seeing that skinny kid who hit me made me think of my father at sixteen. Sean was a mean kid, who came around with his father to tell them they weren't welcome, to move on. There was some pushing then, and a fight, and Sean came at him with a sickle in his hand.

"That boy will never forget me," my father always said in the same words. "Because though he did mark my face right here, the arm that did it will never be straight to do such a deed again."

He looked closely at my eye again, and shook his head. "That's why you've got to do it, boy. You've got to leave your mark on them."

I turned away. This code of my father's made me feel weak in my stomach. This was not my code. No fights. I preferred Mahatma Gandhi. I once saw a picture of that little guy sitting in the middle of the road, blocking a convoy of British armored vehicles, and I realized at once that was me.

"So you should go back out there and settle with whoever did that to you. Whatever bastard ruins you, you should ruin him."

"Okay, father."

"What was his name?"

"I don't know."

"You should find out, and you should find him."

"All I know is he was Irish," I said, just to catch my father's reaction.

"Ahhhh," he said. "Then you have to deal with him. It's a hateful race. It's a race of bigots." He became pensive, as if remembering his own landless people shoved around and persecuted in their homeland. "This is what they understand." He held up his bony fist in my face.

My mother came in, grinning, with a bowl full of butter cookies. Dad relaxed his fist. "My little varnishka," he said. He pulled her down next to him on the couch. "When does *Dagmar* come on?"

"All you want to look at is *Dagmar*. What's wrong with me?"

"I could watch Faye Emerson." He kissed her. "You been digging up the other potatoes while I've been gone?"

"I couldn't tolerate another one," she smiled.

"It's a good thing," he said, and pulled her close.

They loved each other a lot. It was, I realize now, a peculiar relationship. They saw each other only half the year, and maybe that was what made it always fresh. He kissed her and kissed her while I was right there. It made me feel like a million dollars to watch them smooch.

Humboldt Junior High School was a minimum security educational institution. It was a gray school with beige classrooms that had a smell of disinfectant that barely hid the reek of forty years of farting adolescents. It functioned as a holding pen to keep the little animals out of trouble, off the streets. Most of us Bullets were in the special classes for those who would go on to special high schools like Bronx Science or Stuyvesant or Brooklyn Tech, and then maybe to college. I even took Latin there from Mrs. Monforte, the last time it was taught: *amo, amas, amat, amamus, amatis, amant.* She was small and round and dark skinned, and she loved the Latin. I took science from Miss Makarow who liked to hike her skirts up and sit on the boys' desks with her legs crossed (particularly on Zoo's desk, because he was shaving already) as she explained the periodic table. Then there was Mrs. Clayf, our homeroom and English teacher. She had lost a lot of weight quickly, and had a little scrotum of loose flesh that swung from under her chin, and when we messed around in homeroom she would wave her arms in fury and shout, "The bold impertinence of the brazen lot," as the sac under her chin whipped around, and the loose drapes of skin flapped from her arms.

In that school it was dangerous to go to the bathroom, because that was where the power exercised itself. The morning wasn't so bad, but by the sixth or seventh period the bathrooms were full of Fanwoods or Condors smoking cigarettes, and some say drinking beer or whiskey, though I never saw it. Fifteen years later it was probably dope in those bathrooms, but not yet. You walked past the boys' rooms between periods and they just sounded dangerous. The girls were afraid to walk too close to the doors because rumor had it that last year Claudia D'Arcangelo had been pulled inside and lost her virginity there, which once lost is never recovered anywhere. The kids in the special classes, the Bullets, as bad as they needed to go, would hold it in all afternoon, till they got home. That was why I looked at Booby Oserow like he was crazy when he came up to me and Zoo and Stamatakis and Dufner during free period and said, "I want to show you something."

"Show us," I said.

"In the bathroom."

"In the bathroom?"

"What is it? You got a French deck?" Dufner asked.

"Yeah," said Booby, and he pulled a deck of cards from his pocket wrapped in a linen napkin, and folded back a corner to show us.

"He's got a pecker deck," Dufner said.

"Let's go," Stames said.

"Where'd you get it?" asked Zoo.

"My dad's closet. He's got everything in the closet, sunbathing magazines, dirty Popeye comics, everything." Fat Booby was grinning weirdly. He was a pervert in training, son of a pervert dentist. "Let's go in," he said.

We went up to the fifth floor bathroom, which was less likely to be full of the enemy. A couple of kids cleared out when we all went in.

"Come on, let's see it," said Dufner.

The bathroom was gray, with black and white tiles on the floor, and light bulbs covered with chicken wire, and gates on the windows, and it smelled like years of little boys with bad aim at the urinals. Booby shoved the deck under his arm and dropped his pants in front of all of us.

"See. Hormones work," he said.

None of us wanted to look. Maybe his thing had grown, maybe not. His flab still hid it anyway.

"Look at it. Hormones did it."

"Let us see the deck, Booby," said Dufner. He grabbed it from under Booby's arm as Booby pointed at his crotch. The napkin fell to the floor. He held up the first picture. It was in sepia tones, and was hard to see because it looked like it had almost been rubbed off.

"What's happening in that one?" Stames asked.

"I'm getting out of here," said Zoo.

All the pictures were hard to see, and that made it all seem stupid; I mean, you looked at those faded French pictures and wondered who would want to do that anyway. They didn't even look like they were enjoying themselves. The women grimaced like they were at the dentist, and the men had such big things it looked like a job just to haul it around with themselves all the time. I mean some of them looked as big as my arm.

"I'm gonna be that big," said Booby.

"What for? You want to kill your wife?"

Zoo opened the door to leave, and then closed it again real

quick. "Fuck," he said. Zoo almost never said words like that, so I knew it was something serious.

"What is it?" I asked.

"All the Fanwoods are there in the hall. They're waiting for us to come out."

"Hey look at this one," said Dufner, waving a card in the air. It was practically worn out it had been looked at so much.

"Look at those tits. What's she doing? Those are tits, aren't they?"

"She's sucking it," said Booby. "That's what they do in France."

"That's weird," said Stames, pushing the picture away. "Her tits look like douche bags."

"She has to have a big mouth," said Dufner. "She has to practice on potatoes."

"The Fanwoods are out there," Zoo insisted.

"Tell them we're not fighters, we're lovers," said Dufner.

"Sugarman should be here," I said.

"His girlfriend should be here," Dufner said.

"Why are the Fanwoods here?" asked Booby. He took the cards away from Dufner.

"They want to see your deck. Let me borrow your deck," Dufner said.

"I can't. It's my father's."

"I'm a customer," Dufner pointed at his teeth. "Five cavities."

Just then the door flew open and we thought it was the Fanwoods, but it wasn't. In came Mr. Press and Mr. Kutzer, our P.T. teachers.

"Okay, chumps," said Mr. Press. "Why aren't you guys in class? Let's see your passes."

"It's our free period," said Dufner.

"Free period you should be in your homerooms."

"Homeroom is hell," said Dufner. With grown-ups, particularly teachers, he had a hard time controlling himself for his own good.

Kutzer, who could be mean, went for Dufner, but Dufner slipped into a booth and shut the door, so he grabbed me by the shirt and slammed my back against the wall. I mean, I don't really hate anyone, but with Kutzer I came close. His hands were like clamps. "You been smoking." He let me go when he spotted Booby trying to button up his pants after shoving the French deck between his legs. "What are you hiding under your little dick?"

"It's not little," Booby said.

Kutzer yanked down Oserow's pants. "It's a little baby mushroom." The cards scattered all over the floor. "What's the matter, can't you hold it in, fatso?"

Booby was crying. A teacher, even a P.T. teacher, has no right to make a kid cry. Mr. Press picked up the cards. "That's my father's," said Booby.

Kutzer picked up a couple of the cards. "Look at this. Look at these pictures," as if he'd never seen them before. "They belong to Dr. Oserow, to a dentist." He was nasty, a small person. I could see it even then. It made me feel I had the big joke up on him when I learned that Kutz meant vomit in German; I mean, every time I said his name I felt like I'd really faked him out.

Kutzer took the rest of the deck from Mr. Press. "All right, get out of here," said Mr. Press.

"Give that back to me," said Booby, reaching for the deck in Kutzer's hand.

"Ah ah ah ah ah." Kutzer held the dirty pictures up in the air where Oserow couldn't reach. He tried to jump for it but he could only get a couple of inches off the ground.

"They're my father's."

"Don't cry, fatso. Just tell the dentist to come to my office here and I'll give it back to him."

"Kutzer, you're such a prick," said Dufner. I guess I'll always love him a little for that. He wasn't afraid to call a prick a prick.

"I'll see you in my office, Dufner."

"Not if I see you first."

"Okay. Okay, let's go," said Mr. Press.

"We can't go out there, Mr. Press," said Zoo.

"Cut the bullfeathers, and let's go," said Press. "You guys just get back to your homeroom and we'll forget about this."

"The Fanwoods are out there," said Stames.

"What's the Fanwoods? There's no one out there," said Press.

"Mr. Press," I said. "The Fanwoods have been after us for weeks."

Kutzer couldn't get his eyes off the deck. "You don't get out there you'll have more than the Fanwoods after you."

"I guarantee there's no one out there," said Mr. Press. I liked him because he was an honest man. He taught civics and gym. The school had no real gym, just a basement with some lines drawn on the floor, and he did the best he could to give the kids good P.T. He believed in it, that kids needed the physical training. He opened the door, and he was being straight with us. No one was there. The Fanwoods must have left when they saw Press and Kutzer come in. "Okay, chumps. Vamoose." We followed the two teachers back to Mrs. Clayf in the homeroom, because the Fanwoods could be anywhere, waiting for us on any stairway, waiting to bust us up because we were

New York Bullets, because Sugarman was a New York Bullet, because Florry O'Neill was from their side of Broadway.

After school that afternoon I saw Florry O'Neill in Sugarman's jacket standing on the corner, waiting for him to come out and walk her home. She smiled a real nice smile at me as I walked by; I mean a smile that warms up your face; so I turned and went back to talk to her.

"Hi," I said. "Fred coming out?"

"Sure," she said.

"I'm Swanny." I pointed at the name on the jacket. "You mind if I stand here with you for a minute?"

"Sure," she said.

Kutzer came out of the school and crossed the street to where his car was parked. He leaned against the door and looked at us for a minute before he sat down inside. I stood there with her. It was hard for me to say anything at first. This was the first time I had ever really looked at her face. She was so pretty it made me sad. I didn't really understand it then, but I've since come to realize that pretty women have always made me melancholy. There's something so vulnerable, so easily exploitable about the affliction of beauty. Don't get me wrong, I appreciate it, I enjoy a beautiful woman, but the easy wealth of her beauty often gets between herself and being really who she is. Who can resist, in possession of such a gift, of such a marketable commodity, the exploitation of it. And it comes to her so young. It takes an exceptional effort by a remarkable woman to transcend the image she is drawn to project. That's why it has always been painful for me to be in love with a beauty, because she frequently doesn't know herself, doesn't trust herself, doesn't like herself.

Now Florry O'Neill was really pretty, and like I said, I didn't like Irish girls. At the time my idea of pretty was a dark one like Linda Cuebas; but Florry was an exception. Mostly I looked at her eyes; I mean, I tried to look at them because it was scary to look at someone who was really pretty. It will drive you crazy. Who knows what will happen to you? But her eyes were so beautiful, and so strange. One of them was green, and the other was half grey and half brown, like light caramel color. Hard to believe. I looked at them so hard she turned away.

Kutzer was still sitting in his car across the street, with his motor running, looking at us through sunglasses.

"You used to be with Jack Ryan, right?" I asked.

"Sure," she said.

"And now you're going with Fred Sugarman?"

"Sure. What is this, twenty questions?"

It wasn't easy for me to talk to her. I sighed. It was a real deep sigh, like I never felt myself do before, like the sigh Gloria Grahame gave when she was thinking of leaving Humphrey Bogart, the movie writer who the cops are chasing, even though she knows in her heart he is innocent. She was confused. I was confused because I didn't know how to say what I wanted.

"You know the Fanwoods are after us?"

She looked at me with all her eyes, and a faint, compassionate smile came to her lips like a kiss from nowhere. "Sure. I know that."

"It's Ryan who's mad because you and Sugarman are together now, and now you're wearing his jacket, right?"

"Sure. I don't know."

"You know the Bullets don't fight. We're just going to get stomped."

Tears came to her eyes, her beautiful eyes. I didn't want to see her cry, but I wanted to finish talking to her.

"Can't you talk to Jack Ryan?"

"He doesn't talk to me. He never talked to me. He doesn't care."

Sugarman came out of the school and we both watched him walk towards us.

"Look, just talk to him, maybe. It could make things a little better."

"He doesn't listen. He'd tell me to shut up."

"Please, Florry."

Sugarman arrived all grins, looking like one of those puppies whose tail wagged its whole body.

"I do what I want to do," she said just before she hugged Sugarman. Sounded like something my father could have said. They hugged so hard I felt it in my own body; I mean, they were really warm for each other. I was a little jealous of it, but not so much, and the thought crossed my mind that what the hell, we'd fight. It was worth it. This was the pursuit of happiness. This was America—not Poland, or France, or Germany, where the Jews let it come down on themselves. Even if we got our asses kicked we'd keep our respect. So we weren't fighters, I thought. So we'd fight. But then I thought that was stupid. That was the way the world always went. That was the way the atom bomb would get to end the human race. That kind of stupid thinking. I would imitate the little guy and sit down in the road if I had to do it myself. Mahatma Gandhi. I was only half a Jew, anyway. The other half had a feel for the rest of the world.

"Baldeen called a meeting for Saturday morning at my house," Sugarman told me.

"What for?"

"We're going to talk about the game and dance."

"It's basketball. What does he have to do with basketball?"

"He wants to talk about the Kiwanis and the American Legion for next year."

"So what does that have to do with a game and dance at the Y?"

"He's gonna coach basketball now for the Bullets."

"Oh, shit."

"What's wrong with it? He's a good coach. He's mature."

"It makes it all too official. Just because he's almost eighteen doesn't mean he's mature. Why does he want to spend all his time with us kids?" I enjoyed playing basketball. I didn't want to have to work at it for a coach. I looked at Florry as if for sympathy.

"Saturday's the meeting. Be there."

"Are you going to come to the dance?" I asked Florry.

"Sure," she said.

They left, and I watched them walk down the street. I noticed Kutzer's car, that might have been circling the block, follow them, and it turned the corner on 177th Street just when they did. Weird.

I met Zoo walking home to 170th Street. "What do you think," I asked him. "Why does Baldeen want to talk about the dance? You think he wants to skim a little money off it?"

"Nah," Zoo said.

"Well, what?"

"He's just lonely. He hasn't got any friends."

That was a simple explanation. I'd settle for that. "I bet the Fanwoods show up at the dance."

"They never come to dances at the Y."

"They'll come to this one."

"Why?"

"If Florry O'Neill is there. Don't kid me."

"This is bullshit. This is stupid," Zoo said.

"You're right," I said. "But that's the way it is."

The meeting seemed almost too official, like a stupid bunch of grown-ups, just because Baldeen was there. This was a whole different idea of the Bullets, not just some kids who want to play ball. You couldn't even laugh. Baldeen didn't have a sense of humor. I don't think I ever saw him laugh. It was one of those mornings when Stames was farting every minute—real loud ones—but if you let out a laugh afterwards in front of Baldeen you felt like you were committing a crime. Another thing that made the meeting a little different was that Florry was there, a girl at a Bullet meeting. I sort of liked it, but it made us self-conscious at first about our language.

We met at Sugarman's house, in his room, and had to pass his father sitting in the living room in his easy chair in a cloud of pipe smoke, reading a German book, listening to Mozart on WQXR. He didn't look up once as we passed through the room. He drove a city bus for a job, but in real life he was a scholarly gentleman and an amateur philosopher. He surrounded himself at home with music and books, all European culture. He didn't want to hear anything about baseball. Sugarman's mother was a plump, Austrian hausfrau. She brought in a bowl full of cookies and watched us for a minute from the doorway.

"Nice kids," she said. "But remember, Freddie, Nanna is still asleep. Not too much noise."

"I hate my grandmother," Sugarman whispered, after his mother left.

"He just says that," Florry said. "He doesn't hate her." Florry crawled into the back corner of Sugarman's bed and leaned against the wall with her legs crossed under her, and stitched on a hoop of embroidery. I couldn't stop looking her way, just because she was a girl, making her delicate movements. There was something encouraging about it.

Stames and I wanted to get the meeting over with before the first show at the Coliseum, because we wanted to see this movie, *All the King's Men*, which was supposed to be good, and it was playing with a movie called *Babes in Blue*, which wasn't supposed to be so good, but had Marie Windsor in it, and she was going to wear a bikini, so that's the movie we really wanted to see.

Baldeen talked seriously about the next baseball season, through Sugarman's voice mostly, as usual. We should keep in shape, he said, get together three times a week and do push-ups and chins and run some laps. Fat chance, I said to Stames. He talked about ordering our uniforms, at least thirty-five bucks each.

"What kind of millionaires you think we are? You think we got Rockefellers for parents?" Stames asked, and farted for punctuation.

"A team with uniforms is a team, not like a team without them." That was a typical Baldeen stupid wisdom sentence. Made most of the Bullets real quiet; not Stames, however.

"Yeah, it's a team that's broke. You've got to hock your mother's tits."

"Hey, there's a girl in the room, Stames," I whispered to him.

"So what?" Florry didn't even look up from her embroidery.

"You can't play Kiwanis ball without uniforms, not to mention American Legion," said Baldeen through Sugarman's mouth.

"Did anyone talk to Barney about sponsoring us? A sponsor would solve that whole shmear," Schletzbaum said.

"Barney'll never sponsor us," I said. "He's too cheap."

"Why don't you just talk to him? You know him best," Sugarman said to me. "It won't hurt."

"You talk to Jack Ryan. I'll talk to Barney."

Sugarman couldn't meet my eyes when I mentioned Jack Ryan. He looked at Florry and she raised her gaze to the ceiling and shrugged.

"You think we could get the Fanwoods to sponsor us?" Dufner asked. "What do you think, Florry? You think they'll sponsor us?"

Florry slowly looked up at Dufner, and smiled a wicked, winning Irish smile. She put her embroidery down in her lap. "That's a good question," she said. "You should ask them. If you ask them, Frankie, I don't see how they can resist."

"Zoo," Sugarman said. "Why don't you ask Ascot Drugs. You work for them."

"I just work for them. I deliver prescriptions. I don't even think they like baseball. I don't know."

"Ask. How will it hurt?"

"I don't know."

Baldeen whispered in Sugarman's ear again. "Whatever we earn from the game and dance, that can go to the uniforms."

"What do you mean?" Jackobitz whined. "We probably won't even get enough to pay the band. Anyway it was supposed to go for our basketball uniforms."

"Yeah," said his brother, Hubby. "We can't keep playing shirts and skins."

"What band did we decide?" Dufner asked.

"Deuce Douros and the Aces," Sugarman said.

"Vomit," said Dufner.

"Who we gonna play?" Bernie Grossman asked.

"We're gonna play the Royals."

"Who are the Royals?" I asked.

"The Royals with boils," said Dufner.

"They're from the Bronx. Baldeen invited them," Sugarman said.

"Are they any good?" Stamatakis asked.

It is extremely important at a game and dance that you play a team you can beat, so that if girls come to the game they can see how great you are. No one knew anything about the Royals.

"They play baseball in the Kiwanis and came in third last year. We never saw them play basketball, but they're coming here to play us a game and then we'll go there."

"To the Bronx?" Dufner couldn't believe it.

"Yeah."

"I don't go to the Bronx. You can get killed in the Bronx."

"Speaking of getting killed," I said. "What if the Fanwoods come to the dance?"

"They never come to a dance," Jackobitz said.

"Isn't your girlfriend going to be at the dance?" I said to Sugarman.

"So what," he said, looking over at her. "It's a free country." Florry just shook her head, not looking up from what she was doing.

"Sugarman," I said. "You've got shit for brains."

"You should watch your language with a girl here," Grossman said.

Dufner leaned over and put his head next to Sugarman. "Which twin has the Toni?"

Baldeen whispered to Sugarman again.

"Let's get back to uniforms. That's why we're here," Sugarman repeated.

"Up your ass with uniforms, Baldeen," said Stames. "I'm going to the movies."

"C'mon. There's a girl here," Grossman said.

"Your sister's a girl," said Dufner.

"Look," I said. "It's stupid to have a dance if the Fanwoods are going to come around and bust us up. What good is that?"

"I'm not scared of them," said Hubby.

"No one's going to bust us up," said his older brother.

"I'll talk to my father, anyway," Schletzbaum said.

"We'll have cops?" Grossman grinned. "Cops at our dance?" The idea excited him. Something about the protection of his sister's virtue was running through his mind.

"I don't want cops there," Dufner said.

"It's better than Fanwoods," I said.

"There'll be girls there," said Dufner. "What if they want to put out?"

"Girls don't put out at a dance," Grossman said, then glanced at Florry and covered his mouth.

"Your sister does," Dufner said. "Abigail Musselman said she was coming. She stoops for the troops. And so is Audrey Wolfe. I asked her personally."

"You mention my sister just one more time, Dufner. Just once more. Anyway why would Audrey Wolfe come? She's seventeen. She goes out with twenty-year-olds. She ever put out for you?" He whispered that last so Florry didn't have to hear it if she didn't want to.

"Your sister put out for me," Dufner came back.

"Shut up, dammit. How can you talk like that with a girl here?"

"No one says she has to stay. It's a free country. Hey, Florry." He leaned over towards her. "Do girls put out at a dance? Just to settle an argument."

Florry didn't even flinch or blush. She looked right at him. "I can't talk for everyone, Frankie, but if you've got a good personality anything is possible. Girls do whatever they want to do, not what you want them to do."

"And what about if you don't have a good personality?"

"Then you're a jerk. You talk about sports. All boys do is talk, anyway."

I never heard a girl talk like that before. She could stay right with Dufner, and I thought she was shy when I first talked to her. I realized there was a lot I had to learn about girls.

"This is getting too personal," Stames stood up. "Swanny and me are going to see *Babes in Blue* and that other movie. See you later, alligator."

I guess the meeting broke up after we left. We walked along Fort Washington to 181st Street. It was a perfect day to go to the movies—murky, drizzling—slicker and umbrella weather. We stopped at the Hebrew National Deli on 181st for a hot dog. The owner was a big Russian guy with a beard and a little wife bent like a hook, who ran around double time doing most of the work, and singing in Russian, or Turkish, or Roumanian.

"Hey," Stames whispered to me. "What do you think? You think maybe they'd want to sponsor the Bullets?"

"We can ask. You want to ask?"

Stames leaned forward on the counter. The Russian was shifting hot dogs on his grill, and turning the knishes over. He had rings on every finger. "Hey, Mr. Hebrew."

"You kids want another hot dog?"

"No. But can I ask you a question?"

"You a couple of wise guys?"

"No, Mr. Hebrew. Not us. We just want to ask a question."

"You kids are wise guys. I know kids."

"Mr. Hebrew, we're from the New York Bullets Social and Athletic Club," Stames pointed at the B on his jacket. "And we wondered if you would want to sponsor us."

"Did you look at the kugel, Sadie?" he shouted to his wife who had just set a tray of baked apples down on the other end of the counter. "Usually we don't open on Saturdays," he told us. "But what can you do? We need the business. What do you want from me?"

"We wondered if you want to sponsor our baseball team."

"Get away from me."

"You get advertising. We put your business name on our uniforms. We buy all our hot dogs here."

"I don't need this. You boys want another hot dog, or what?"

"Sure," said Stames. The Russian flipped another special into a bun. "But I don't have another quarter."

"Okay, boys. Wise guys." He threw the hot dog back onto the grill. "You finished eating. You don't want another hot dog. Go away. Go away, boys." The Russian walked back to the door of the kitchen. "Sadie," he shouted, and then he shouted something in Russian.

We opened the door to leave. Stames turned back just as we stepped out, "Give me some old lady's tit on pumpernickel.

Make it an onion roll." The Russian came at us past the tables like a big bear.

"Struck out there," said Stames, as we trotted to the Coliseum through the mist.

In our neighborhood there were two big theaters. One was the Loew's 175th Street, which was really fancy, decorated like a Chinese Palace. It was the greatest experience of your life to go to the movies there, because you came off the street into another world—walked through the big brass doors onto the oriental carpets, among the giant fake Chinese vases, everything in the lobby burnished in a coppery light—and then you went to your seat, and they even had someone playing an organ sometimes, and you sat down, and it got dark, and then it was so great, the thrill of a cool breeze across your mind. It was the movies. The Loew's shut down early in the sixties, and then was bought by Reverend Ike, and turned into a temple for his money worship. The RKO Coliseum was the other big theater, and that had no particular theme of decoration, but a rich movie-theater smell and a kind of silvery light throughout it. The balcony of the Coliseum had a reputation for kids making out in it, and although we didn't mention it to each other both Stames and I had that a little bit in mind.

You went to the movies to stay all day. Some kids would see the double feature three times. The best I ever did was two-and-a-half double features when *Treasure of Sierra Madre* was playing, then I went again during the week after school and watched it again. If I was going to be Mahatma Gandhi, I thought, I would be an American one and have a stubbly face and talk like Humphrey Bogart. I never liked another movie as much until *The African Queen*, even though the movie I saw that day really stirred me up—*All the King's Men*. I always hated to

see little guys get the shaft from big politicians, and maybe
that movie influenced me in my idealism to become a lawyer—
as I am unfortunately today—spreading the cheeks of the law,
as I discovered you need to do in New York City to survive,
and to do just a little good. Anyway, me and Stames watched
Babes in Blue, in which Marie Windsor did once get out of her
Wave uniform and into a bikini and got all the swabs hot and
bothered. Then we watched Broderick Crawford turn into a
ruthless bastard, and then we went up to the balcony.

After you saw both movies you went up to the balcony to
see if there were any girls there. Usually some girls were
there. If two girls came together they usually sat with a seat
between them so some boys could sit down too. Sometimes a
bunch of girls would come and they'd sit in different seats all
over the balcony. It was the closest thing in our neighborhood
to paradise on Saturday afternoon. What you did was walk
around the balcony till you saw someone you wanted to try to
sit near, and then you sat down in the same row two or three
seats away from her and waited for a signal, which was she
could cross her legs and glance at you and give you a little
smile. Or she could pretend she was uncomfortable in her seat
and move over one seat closer to you, and then you could close
the gap. You moved to the seat right next to her. Then there
were crucial moments when you both shifted around, and
exchanged some peculiar smiles, and pretended to watch the
movie you had seen already maybe twice. Then you'd slowly
start your strategy. You could stretch your arms out and
yawn, and your arm that was next to her would fall to the
back of her seat as if it were doing it by itself, and your hand
would brush her shoulder. She'd look down at that hand and
wrinkle her brow and then look at you, and that was when

you had to put a little pressure on her shoulder, not too much
so she'd think you were really doing it, but enough so if she
really wanted to she could lean a little your way. It was all
strategies in the balcony. If she leaned closer then after a
minute or two you could turn your face and kiss her. Then
you pulled back and looked at her and said something like,
"What's your name?"

"I'm Mary."

"My name is Swanny," I said.

"You a Fanwood?" one of the Maries asked me once. She
couldn't see the color of my jacket in the dark.

"I'm a Bullet," I said, pointing at the B above my heart.

"Excuse me," she said, and she stood up to leave. It was like
I'd told her I had leprosy.

"Don't forget your jacket," I said, but she was gone. I don't
know if she ever came back for the jacket. That was enough
for me. I left the theater. She probably went to Incarnation,
and the Fanwoods made the Bullets out-of-bounds for the
Maries from the Catholic school.

But if the first kiss worked out, the second one was supposed to be a French kiss. That seemed weird to me, at first; I
mean, who wanted to put his tongue inside some girl's
mouth? Some of them had braces. Some had B.O. and bad
breath. But you had to do it if you wanted to go the next
step, which was to cop a feel, which was possible if the girls
had real tits. She was usually waiting for it, and I met one
once who moved my hand right onto herself. It was pretty
big and I liked squeezing it, though after a while it seemed
silly. But if the girl had falsies on she wouldn't let you get
near her. "What God Has Forgotten We Stuff With Cotton."
Who wanted to squeeze some cotton anyway? That was it,

our big thrills. In the Coliseum balcony nothing was allowed below the waist.

Anyway Stames and I went up there and it was pretty empty except there was one girl sitting alone in the second row, where Stames sat down, and the one I sat down next to was sitting with her friend in about the seventh row. I got my hand onto her shoulder and she sat there real straight. She wore a nice soft sweater that I liked to touch, but underneath she was stiff as a door.

"Am I bothering you?" I asked.

"No," she said, real quick, without looking at me. She took a cigarette out of her little purse and stuck the end of it into her mouth in the middle of her lipstick.

"Do you want me to leave?" I asked.

"No," she said, and lit the cigarette, and started puffing on it. Mamoulian smoked cigarettes like a chimney, and he was always trying to get the other Bullets to smoke them, but I never did, and I'm grateful for it. This girl sat there puffing the cigarette in the middle of her face. The idea of kissing a cigarette mouth wasn't very appealing. And a French kiss? Like licking out a dirty ash tray.

"What's your name?" I asked.

"What's it to you?" she said.

"Nothing," and I took my arm away from the back of her seat. "You want me to leave?"

"No," she said, "I don't," and she turned her head to look at me, and she grabbed my hand. Sucking on the cigarette in the middle of her face she looked like some kind of weird fish. I don't think she was older than twelve.

"How old are you?" I asked.

"Sixteen," she said. She held onto my hand and wrist as if it was the bar in front of her seat on the Cyclone at Coney Island. I sat there and watched *Babes in Blue* some more, my arm falling asleep on NoName's lap. She put out her cigarette. I didn't want to kiss her now. Stames looked like he was making out fine in the second row, the girl smothered under his big body. I almost forgot the girl sitting next to me.

"My name is Mary," she said.

"That's a good name," I said.

"Thanks, I'm sure," she said.

"My sister's name is Mary," I said.

"What's your name?" she asked.

"Jack." I don't know why I said it. She might have known him. "Jack Ryan."

"No. You're kidding me." The friend on her left was blowing a bubble so big she couldn't see the movie. Mary jabbed her with her elbow. "This is Jack Ryan. I got Jack Ryan here," she whispered to her friend.

The friend turned her bubble to look at me and breathed, sucking a pink veil of bubble gum against her face. She stared at me through her one free bubble gum eye. "I'm gonna die. I can't stand it," she said.

I saw about six guys come down the steps of the balcony and sit down behind Stames. It looked strange, but I didn't think about it at first because they weren't wearing Fanwood jackets or anything. What could I do anyway if there was trouble, just me? Pretty soon I saw that there was something going on. They had leaned over Stames and were closed on him like flies on a smear of syrup. Should I have gone down there, just me? I don't know what I could have done. It all happened very quickly. In a second they had picked him up and were dragging him up the aisle. It was scary. That could have been me, but they always seemed to like to pick on Stames first, because he was so big. I was lucky. There was no one behind me. Stames would have been screaming his head off except they had a gag in his mouth. Where were the ushers? They hustled him up the balcony. Where were the damned police?

"What's going on, Jack," Mary asked.

"The Howdy Doody Show," I said. I got up and started for the aisle.

"Jack, are you coming back?" The wistfulness in her voice was so delicious I wanted to stay and be Jack Ryan forever, to taste some more of his power.

"You stick around, Mary," I said, and I followed the huddle with Stames in the middle down to the mezzanine lobby. It's like there was never a cop or an usher in the world. All you have to do is put your feet up on the back of a seat and twenty ushers appear, but when real trouble comes up in the Coliseum—not a uniform.

I didn't know if these were Fanwoods or what. Maybe they were Solomons, but with their reputation of Robin Hood you wouldn't expect them to do something like this. Maybe they were just some guys on a mean rampage and they had planted a girl friend as bait. They pushed Stames into the bathroom, and I stood there near the door. I could hear the newsreel go on in the theater. *The March of Time.* I could hear the guys laughing and scuffling in the john. I thought of running for the police, but I knew police don't take a kid seriously. By the time I could explain it, by the time I could get them to listen to me and come, it would be over. Why was I standing there? Maybe I was just curious. Morbid curiosity.

I leaned around and peeked in. They all were crowded

around one toilet stall, grunting and laughing, as if they were ducking for apples. What was happening was they were having trouble turning Stames over, he was so big. Jesus, I thought, that could have been me. They could have flipped me over in a second and swirled my head in the toilet bowl. Stames was fighting it with all his big strength. One of the kids flew back against the sink. "Come on. Come on," he said, running back into it. "Get the bastard down."

I should have jumped in there and battled with them, but I knew that would have made it worse. When it comes to fighting, I think too much.

"Just let them do it, Stames. Just let them. Then you won't get hurt. Please," I mumbled. I heard him roar through his gag, and I stepped into the doorway. I could have run in there and jumped on one of their backs, but then we both would have got killed. I thought about it, and I stood there. Finally Stame's feet went up in the air, and I heard the toilet flush. What a relief. They dropped Stames in the booth, and I flattened back against the wall as they all ran out of the bathroom. One of them threw a punch as he ran by me, and missed. I approached Stames slowly, who was on his knees, throwing up around the gag into the toilet bowl. I put my hand on his back and felt him stiffen up.

"It's me. It's Swanny."

I untied his hands and he pulled the gag out of his mouth and let it all go into the toilet. Popcorn, coke, and chocolate babies. I brought him some paper towels and he sat up on the toilet seat and didn't look at me.

"Are you okay?"

He shook his head.

"You think those guys were Fanwoods?"

He just sighed, and started to sob. He was crying. Stamatakis was one of those kids who never cried.

"I want to know where the ushers were. Where were they?"

"Fuck you," he said.

"Come on, Stames. What could I do?" I felt like a jerk,
Stames there on the toilet and crying, his vomit splotching his
chest.

"Fuck you. Just go away."

"What if they come back? You better get out of here,
Stames."

"Leave me alone. Just go away. Fuck you."

"Come on. Let's go." I tried to pull him by the arm, but he
pushed me out of the booth.

"Fuck you. Fuck you, Swanny. Fuck everyone."

I left the bathroom. What could I do? I checked the mezzanine and balcony for those guys. No sign of them. Mary and
her friend were still sitting there. I guessed it would be okay to
leave Stames alone like he wanted to be. I could feel in my gut
how humiliating it had been for him. I could feel it as if it was
myself, how impotent. I had a yellow streak in me that must
have been a mile wide. Yeah I should have jumped in, should
have got myself messed up and killed. That would have been
stupid, but I would have felt better for it.

Luckily the rain was coming down in buckets outside, so
those kids probably wouldn't be waiting for anyone. Stames
could get home safe without me, and what good could I be to
him anyway. I felt awful. I was nobody. Less than that. I
walked in the middle of the rain and let myself get soaked. I
deserved pneumonia.

I got as far as Zooky's candystore and stopped there for an
egg cream. Zooky and Molly, his wife, worked this candystore

on Broadway off 174th Street. They sold newspapers, comic books, magazines. They had all the candy and a soda fountain. They'd make you a sandwich or heat you a can of soup. They had danishes and pound cake and bagels. It was a comfortable place to pass some time at a counter. Usually there'd be a couple of old guys sitting there drinking coffee and nibbling on a prune danish. They made the best egg cream on Broadway; that is, when Zooky himself did it. His wife was stingy with the syrup, and didn't top the glass off after it foamed up. From Zooky himself you got your money's worth, a full glass. So what you did was wait till his wife was in back before you ordered. He was a bald guy, and he was almost blind, with thick glasses, and he'd pick the egg cream up after he made it and bring it right up to his face, as if doing a quality check, and then he'd put it down in front of you, saying, "You got yourself a Zooky special, sonny."

"Zooky special," his wife would sometimes say. "Special to lose us money."

I just wanted to sit there with an egg cream and forget what happened. Music to put you to sleep was on the radio, some Brahms or Mantovani. I sipped on the egg cream and watched Molly stir mayonnaise into the tuna salad. She could make one can of tuna stretch from here to Philadelphia. And she was a real ugly woman—a good thing Zooky could hardly see her— with a big mole on her chin with long hairs growing out of it. She wore the same green sweater, winter and summer, over a patched blue apron. Sometimes she cackled so weird you expected her to fly out the door on a broom. It was a few weeks from Halloween, and they had masks and cardboard skeletons hanging all over the store. She looked right at home.

I tried to stretch the last third of my egg cream to avoid

going home, where my mother was definitely going to go through her, "How-can-you-stay-in-the-movie-so-long-you're-going-to-ruin-your-eyes" routine. Dinnerman came into the store and sat down next to me. He spun around on the stool a couple of times. Somehow his face looked very sad, like he might have been crying. Whenever I thought my life might be bad I thought about Dinnerman. I didn't know too much about him, but I could guess that he had a hard time.

"So what's with the Bullets?" he asked.

"Nothing," I said. "We've got a game and dance in a few weeks at the Y."

"Are the Fanwoods still after you?"

"Fuck it," I said.

"What the Bullets should do is go after them. That's the best way. You should go over to Highbridge and jump them right there. Kick their asses first, that's the best defense."

I looked at him with a feeble smile.

"I don't kid you. I'll go with you."

I looked down in my glass at the suds, and sucked at them with my straw.

"I make that offer," said Dinnerman.

"Didn't your mother tell you not to do that?" Molly said to me. "An elephant in a circus does that." She set an egg salad sandwich on a hard roll in front of Dinnerman.

"Mind your business, Molly," said Zooky. "Leave the kids alone. She's a busybody. She minds everybody's business but her own."

"Kids today," said Molly, scratching herself under the sweater.

"Do I get a pickle or what?" asked Dinnerman. Molly looked at him as if he had insulted her religion.

"You want a pickle," said Zooky. "Here's a pickle." He laid a whole dill pickle on the plate next to the sandwich.

"You don't give a whole pickle. You give a slice," Molly said.

"Molly. Molly. Molly." Zooky walked up and hugged and kissed her. It took a blind man to kiss someone so ugly.

"Yeah, you kiss, but you wonder why you're losing your shirt."

Zooky came back to us, grinning, and tugging on his shirt. "You like my shirt? You want it?"

"See, if they think you're afraid, they'll play with you," Dinnerman said, licking flecks of egg salad off his lips. "Like a cat plays with a mouse. You just got to show them that you're not chicken, that they can't have fun and mess with you."

"Dinnerman." I turned towards him and flapped my arms like wings. *"Bk bk bk bk bk bk bk."* I clucked like a chicken.

He exploded a laugh that sprayed egg salad across the counter onto the mirror over the sink.

"Get out of my store," Molly shouted. An old couple opened the door and stepped inside. "Leave my store, you hoodlums, you Nazis." The old couple backed out into the street. Zooky grabbed Molly by the shoulders and walked her to the back of the store, where she started to cry. Dinnerman was still laughing.

"You didn't look that happy when you came in here," I said to him. We listened to Molly sobbing in the back. "Weird," I said.

"Yeah," he said, and sucked some egg salad off his finger that he'd wiped off his plate. "My fuckin' mother. I'd be okay if I didn't have to have a mother. She's got a boyfriend she calls Boot and he comes in this afternoon with a fuckin' chip on his shoulder. I'm sittin' in my room, and I can hear that he's drunk and I think I hear him take a swing at my mother. It's the worst. I hear her scream and I come out of my room and tell him that if he touches her I'll kill him. I will, Swanny. Fuckin' Boot. I'll kill him. He staggers after me, and I shove him down on the couch and slap his ugly face a couple of times. What the fuck do I know, Swanny? As soon as I reach eighteen I'm gonna join the fuckin' Army."

"You want to go to Korea?"

"I'll join the Navy. You think Korea is World War III?"

"I don't know. I hope not."

"Nah. It can't be. There's a world war every twenty years, and it hasn't even been ten yet."

I swung off my stool.

"Where are you going?" Dinnerman asked.

"Home," I said.

He grabbed my arm. "You're okay. Swanny. Most of the Bullets are wimps, but you're okay."

I have to admit I was flattered even at the expense of my buddies. Dinnerman was seventeen, after all. And he was a guy with grown-up problems, and a survivor.

"Look, why don't you come down to Times Square with me?"

"Times Square?" I'd never been there at night.

"Yeah. I'm going. I go there on Saturday nights."

"What do you do down there?"

"I don't know. It's something to do. It's great there. All kinds of people. You can hang out at Grant's. Hamburgers—twelve cents, Birch Beer—a nickel. We'll see what's there. If things look right I pick up a queer and go to a hotel room and make some money."

"A queer? What do you do?"

"I don't do anything. I don't like queers." He pulled a sap out of his pocket, some lead weights wrapped in soft wool. He put it in my hand. It felt like it was alive, could lift up by itself, like a lead snake.

"A man's best friend," said Dinnerman. "Sometimes it makes me a hundred bucks off an old queer. They've got money."

"You'll be in real trouble doing that some day, Dinnerman." I gave him back his blackjack.

"What's he gonna say? I'm a queer, and this kid stole my money? He's gonna tell that to the cops? The trick is to pick your queers, Swanny. Just come with me once. You'll learn something."

"I think my dad is home," I lied. I knew he'd gone back to South Carolina on "business" and was gone for a couple of weeks. Maybe he was rolling queers himself down there. "I gotta go."

"C'mon," said Dinnerman. "We won't roll the queers. We'll just. . . . We can go to Luigi's and eat spaghetti. We can sit in Bickfords. There are these niggers in there every Saturday night, and they dress like women. You can't even tell the difference. It's a great fake-out. Come on with me."

All that stuff sounded weird; I mean, talking to Dinnerman opened your eyes. Compared to him most of the kids in my neighborhood walked around blindfolded. It was like some grown-up life he was talking about, that I would eventually understand, as I have understood almost too well now, because one of my clients is a Puerto Rican queen who works on Wall Street as a runner, and another is a black transsexual who sells nickel bags in the garment district; but at fourteen and a half I wasn't ready for it. I was scared, in fact.

"I'll go with you some other time, Dinnerman," I said. "My mother will kill me if I don't come home tonight."

"You should kill your mother," he said, as I left the candystore.

My bowels were rumbling around as I walked the rest of the way home. I walked fast because I knew if I didn't get home right away I would drop a load in my pants. I mean, all I'd ever done with a girl before was cop a feel in the Coliseum balcony, and I didn't even get the thrill out of that I was supposed to. So to go down to 42nd Street and mess with some queers with Dinnerman wasn't something I was brave enough to do right then. I mean, what if I liked them? Jesus, I thought, as I threw open the door of the apartment and without shutting it ran for the bathroom. "What if I like queers?" and I dropped my pants, and as I sat down I thought about poor Stames, and I exploded like a time bomb into the toilet.

"Kiddo, I'll tell you something," said Barney. "This has always been a peaceful spot."

"Barney, to sponsor us all you have to do is pay half the uniforms."

"What I'm saying is every year this neighborhood becomes more like a war zone. Now you hear about these Puerto Rican gangs coming up here with their switchblades and zip guns; but I'll tell you, right here next to the park it's a peaceful place by the subway station. We get the occasional nuts here, but what do you expect, it's a big city. Up on Broadway, with all the lights and gates on the storefronts, they still get broken into, robbed. Here it's okeydokey. I sell some newspapers, some candy."

"Some bubblegum too, black market."

"You remember the wartime? You want some bubblegum?"

"Barney, you sponsor us, you get the name of your store printed on every uniform. We win the Kiwanis, you win too." I was waiting at Barney's to meet Zoo, and I figured since I was right there, nothing ventured, nothing gained.

"What do I need it here, to win something? Look, I'll tell you something, frankly. I think the Bullets are nice kids. The cream of the neighborhood. Nice kids, smart kids, but they've got themselves in a little trouble with Sugarman and his shicksa. There are a lot of nice Jewish girls he can go out with. Why does he pick a Florry? A Florry O'Neill?"

"Why must we be teenagers in love?" I sang.

"What's that?"

"Nothing, Barney. It's a free country, you know."

"So frankly, Mr. Swanson, as far as to sponsor you goes, I wish I could. But one, this is a small business and I can't afford it, and I don't need the advertising, and two, I would prefer the Bullets didn't hang around here any more. There's going to be trouble. Those kids from Incarnation are going to come down here, all because of one Irish girl, but also because trouble happens. That's what trouble is. And I'd rather it didn't happen around here. I don't want to die before we retire to Florida." Barney retreated into the darkness of the cave of his newsstand.

I saw Zoo now coming up Fort Washington. His Bullet jacket looked really good. When you wear purple and gold, and you see someone else wearing it, that makes you feel great, like there's someone else with you on the streets. We were meeting because I had convinced Zoo to come with me over to Highbridge Park where the Fanwoods hung out, where I hoped I might do some good talking to Jack Ryan. What did we have to lose? A lot. But if just the two of us walked into their territory they probably wouldn't smash us right away. They'd be surprised, I figured. Besides there was a certain etiquette to these wars. And if I was wrong, we would get stomped. I guess I was ready for that. It was for the general good.

"I don't know about wearing our jackets," said Zoo. "It might be asking for trouble."

"Just to go over there is asking for trouble, Zoo. I think we've got to wear our jackets, Zoo. Otherwise they'll think we're spies." I'd seen a lot of war movies.

We stopped at Zooky's for an egg cream. Neither of us was anxious to get there. Zooky's wife wasn't there, so he was bumping around trying to do everything himself. Poor guy was almost blind, but he could laugh at himself, and he had the whole store memorized by touch. The store seemed much brighter and happier when he was there alone.

"I'm going to train these roaches," he said, "to get Seeing Eye roaches."

Zoo and I talked and talked about where we were going to go to high school, a conversation we had had many times, felt comfortable with. Just a delaying tactic.

Zoo always seemed more mature, older than anyone else, because he looked that way, and he knew what he wanted to be when he grew up. He always wanted to be a pharmacist, and that's why I was surprised when I found out he was a radio announcer, then a TV broadcaster. He learned about that in college.

"If I get a choice," he said, "I'll probably go to Science, but Stuyvesant would be okay. I don't think I want to go to Brooklyn Tech. It's in Brooklyn."

"I'm going to Stuyvesant," I said. "If I get in. You go to the morning session, then you can get a job in the afternoon."

"They're starting to accept girls at Science," said Zoo. "That's going to make it harder to get in."

"Yeah, girls," I said. "Creepy ones. Brainy girls. Stuyvesant will never let girls in."

"Don't you like girls?"

"Yeah. I like them. Stuyvesant has a sister school, Washington Irving. They have dances. It's hard to study with girls in your class."

"I still think Science is a better school."

"The kids are all brains. They all look like walking science projects. Creepy. You can always tell someone from Science. He looks like Ginzy the Creep."

"You're just prejudiced, Swanny."

"Maybe. But at least Stuyvesant is in Manhattan. You don't have to go to the Bronx to get there."

"What's wrong with it? The Bronx has the best zoo in the city, the best botanical garden. It's got the biggest parks. We're gonna play a lot of games in the Bronx next season."

Suddenly we were silent, and we recognized the same apprehension in each other's eyes. Anything to delay crossing Broadway and heading for Amsterdam Avenue. It was like going to our first Regents exam. You just didn't want to enter that room. Or it was like Gary Cooper. *High Noon.* Like someone was going to have to die, even though we knew no one was going to have to die.

"What if you don't get accepted? What if you have to go to G.W.?" G.W. was George Washington, the local high school, where we'd have to go if we didn't get in to one of the special schools. It's where most of the Fanwoods would go to high school.

Zoo shrugged his shoulders. "So I'll go to G.W. It's in the neighborhood. Keep me off the subway."

"The Fanwoods will be at G.W."

Zooky came over and leaned close to us so he could see. "You kids got a baseball team?"

"Yeah," I said.

"Next year we'll be in the Kiwanis and the American Legion," said Zoo. "We've got a manager."

"What do you call yourselves?"

"We're the New York Bullets Social and Athletic Club," I turned around to show him the name on the back of my jacket.

"Bullets? You're such nice boys. Why are you the Bullets?"

"What's wrong with Bullets?"

"Nothing. Just Bullets gives a certain idea."

"What should we call ourselves? The Pigeons? The Classics?"

"Yeah. Something nice."

"Maybe The Brains," Zoo laughed.

"The Brains, why not?" said Zooky. "If you got brains, what's the disgrace?"

"In this neighborhood you don't call yourself a brain," I explained. "Not at our school."

"Tell me, you got a baseball team?"

"Yeah. We told you."

"You got someone to sponsor you?"

Zoo and I looked at each other. He was grinning a mile. I tried to keep myself straight.

"We've got a couple of stores interested. Barney said something," I said.

"Barney's a shylock. I don't want to say anything. Maybe you should let me sponsor you."

"You want to?" Zoo said.

"You have to put ZOOKY'S on your uniforms."

"Zooky, we'll think about it," I said, like a big deal. "Anyway what would your wife say?"

"My wife. What does my wife know from Joe DiMaggio? Maybe there's a new DiMaggio on these Bullets. Even a Dom Dimaggio. A Hank Greenberg. He's Jewish. My wife, if she ever had any children she'd be a different woman."

We left it at that for the time being, told Zooky we'd come back later to talk about it. We stepped out of the store, and stood on Broadway in front of it, feeling a certain kind of elation. Now we had to cross Broadway and venture into Fanwood territory.

"I don't know if I can go through with this," I said to Zoo. The egg cream felt like it was still fizzing in my stomach.

"Come on, Swanny," said Zoo. "This was your idea. Look at the sunshine today. Let's go."

We went. In upper Manhattan Broadway separates two different kinds of territory. West of the longest avenue in the world there were hills falling towards the Palisades and towards the Hudson, like 173rd Street was a steep hill from Broadway to Fort Washington Avenue, and a rise and fall from Ft. Wash to Haven Avenue, which was right on the edge of the Palisades cliffs. These hills were great for sledding in the winter, where every year some kid got hurt riding his new Flexible Flyer into the traffic. East of Broadway the streets flattened out towards the Harlem River. The buildings west of Broadway were big and broad and usually had courtyards in front, and elevators. They looked more like white-collar brick palaces than the five- and six-story walk-ups to the east, that gave the feeling of being slightly tenement. I don't think the rents were much different one side or the other, but there was a separation, like low-level accountants and office managers to the west, and blue-collar construction and subway workers, firemen, cops, to the east, although obviously that wasn't absolute, because Schletzbaum's father was a detective, and he lived west on 173rd, and Grossman's father was a subway conductor. I'm just talking looks.

We walked east on 175th Street past Audubon Avenue to St. Nicholas Avenue. St. Nich wasn't so bad for Bullets, although it was best not to wear your jacket there, and you had to be careful. But Woolworth's was on St. Nich between 179th and 180th, and we shopped there, so we were used to walking that avenue—at least the west side of it—in ordinary clothes. It was touchy, but it was normal. The big threat, the scare, was to cross to the east side of St. Nich and head down any street towards Amsterdam. This was like entering the dark woods, like you wanted to sprinkle crumbs so you could find your way out, or maybe it was like Billy Batson first felt running from the crooks down the abandoned subway station in the comic book, passing the statues of the Seven Deadly Sins, to the end where he finally met Shazam, whose name, just by saying it, caused a flash of lightning, and turned a lame newsboy into the all-powerful Captain Marvel. A little kid getting the power. I always felt more for him than for Clark Kent.

We didn't see any kids on the block going towards Amsterdam Avenue, only one old guy with an old white mangy dog stumbling along, and a couple of ladies pulling their shopping carts towards the Broadway A & P. Near the corner of Amsterdam some girls were sitting on a stoop. When they saw our jackets they got up and disappeared around the corner, so that's where we figured the Fanwoods were. The sky over

Highbridge Park, over the Harlem River, was bright blue, full of cotton balls of clouds. Big trucks ran up Amsterdam Avenue.

"Wait a second," Zoo grabbed my arm. "What do we do when we see them? What if they're right around the corner there?"

"What do you mean what do we do?"

"Do we walk right up to them? Do we wait for them to come to us? Do we cross the street? We don't have any strategy."

"I don't know. We'll just see what happens."

"Shit," said Zoo, something he almost never said.

"What?" I said.

Zoo looked embarrassed.

"What?"

"I've got to go. I've got to go bad."

"No. Number one or number two?" I asked.

"I don't know. Both."

"Can't you hold it in? You've got to hold it in."

He gave me a weak smile. "I guess so."

We started for the corner again, and first we saw one guy step out in a black and silver jacket. He looked big. He stood there with his hands on his hips like the Colossus of Rhodes and looked at us, then made a gesture to some others still hidden around the corner, and the black jackets started to flow into the space around the corner lamppost like hot tar. Zoo froze.

"Don't stop." I placed my hand inconspicuously in the small of his back to push him on. "Keep walking slow. Don't look scared," I said with my mouth closed. I don't think I sounded real convincing. I was scared enough myself. I tried to push him along, but he was frozen in place.

"Shit," he said. "I can't hold it in."

"Try to smile a little."

"I'm sorry, Swanny." Zoo turned and ran back down the street; I mean, he disappeared in the distance, gone like a bullet. Now I saw him, now I didn't. A fast kid. Stole many bases in the Kiwanis. I never blamed him myself. I was a jerk to stay there in my Bullet jacket alone. Later he told me that what went through his mind was: "I don't want to shit in my pants. I want to go to college. I want to be a pharmacist. I don't want to die."

I would have run, but my muscles wouldn't let me. It was weird. I was too scared to run. All the Fanwoods were there like the black plague, and I was some stupid kid stuck in a purple and gold jacket. There was nothing else to do. The Fanwoods watched me walk slowly into their midst. They were saying things to me, but for all I could get through my panic they could have been talking Gaelic. I was right in the middle of all of them, like spinning in a whirlpool. I was so dizzy the air kept changing color, yet I could stand up. Maybe this was what fear was like. I didn't know. I was not myself for those moments. That for a long time I didn't say anything must have made an impression. I looked down, and that little mascot kid who had picked on Stames and then on me in my courtyard was being bratty, though at first I didn't hear a word of his. "Unitarian. Unitarian," I finally heard him say, the first words that came through. So he remembered me. I wanted to say what I had to say but I was waiting for my voice to find its way onto my tongue. I opened my mouth, and no words came out. Nothing.

"Hey. Nice jacket. I like your jacket, but I think there's a pussy in it," said the biggest one, the one who had come around the corner first; I mean, this guy was so big you had to say his name twice. Kevin was on his jacket. Kevin Kevin. He stepped up and put a hand on my jacket. "Let me wear your jacket."

I still couldn't say anything.

"Hey the pussy can't talk. Are you a Bullet pussy? A great big Bullet? Pussy pussy. Gimme your jacket. I want to be a Bullet." He pulled on my jacket. I stepped away from him, and something in me, like some insight from the future made me realize that even though he was big he was just a kid like me, this Kevin with green eyes. He was big but he had acne, Kevin Kevin.

"I'll trade jackets with you, Kevin," I said. "You can wear mine if I can wear yours." I took off my jacket and placed it in his hands. Kevin Kevin looked startled, as if I'd done something totally amazing. The kids gathered around him to look at the jacket, and reached out to touch it as if it was made of paradise feathers.

"Let him wear your jacket, Kevin," one kid said.

"Your name is Swanny, huh? Swanny?" He looked in my eyes as if it was the first time he had seen me. "Swanny River. Okay." He stripped off his jacket and handed it to me.

"Okay, Kevin," I said, putting on his jacket, in which seven of me could have lived without ever seeing each other, and he looked like the fat guy in Smilin' Jack comics who was always popping buttons off his shirt because he was so big.

"Look at me now," said Kevin Kevin. "I'm a cute little Bullet." He walked around, swinging his hips. The girls who were on the stoop started to giggle.

"Hey, Kevin," said another Fanwood. "Don't make me pop a boner." The laughter loosened the gang up and they started to spread out, and didn't stare at me so much, but watched the big boy flit around in my little jacket. I watched him too, and I was laughing, even though the laugh was supposed to be on me.

Another of the Fanwoods, a red-headed kid who wasn't laughing, who probably didn't ever think anything was funny stepped up to me and grabbed the Fanwood jacket I was wearing. Bill was the name of his jacket. "What are you doing here, Bullet faggot?" Bill asked.

"I came to talk to Jack Ryan."

"You think you can come here and talk to Ryan?"

"I don't know. I just came here to see if I could talk to him."

"Stay here." He let go of my jacket and walked to the corner and looked down the street, then came back. "You come alone?" he asked.

"No," I said. "I brought my father."

"What's your name?"

"Swanny."

"Both your names."

"William Swanson."

"What's your nationality?"

I'd heard that question before, and figured I'd better go straight to it this time. "My father's Irish and my mother's Jewish."

He looked at me as if he thought that was impossible, as if I was talking about life on a different planet. He looked around as if to find some other Fanwoods to help him out, but they had followed Kevin Kevin up the street. For the first time I saw the trashed up alien storefronts of Amsterdam Avenue. Most of them were empty. There was a machine shop, a junk store of some kind, a hardware store covered with a steel gate so you didn't know if it was ever open or not. This was another way of life. Like I said, you always have something to learn about your own neighborhood. This made Broadway look like Fifth Avenue. And across Amsterdam were the big pillared entrances of Highbridge Park, with its swimming pools, closed now, its giant wrought iron gates locked shut, its gloomy brick facade full of shadows. Anywhere you looked up or down this avenue you didn't see one candystore.

"Why do you want to talk to Ryan?" Bill asked.

"I thought we could talk about the Bullets and the Fanwoods. I wanted a discussion about what's going on."

A little grin sneaked onto this Bill's face, and he rubbed his hands together. "Are we gonna rumble?" he asked, holding up his fist right under my chin. That gesture was almost friendly. He was smiling at the prospect of the fight. That was as friendly as this kid got. I didn't answer him. I didn't have a very convincing vocabulary for fighting. At least I was smart enough to keep quiet. That has always been a gift I've had. Silence. To know when to shut up, and how.

"Come on," he said. "Come with me." We walked to the other end of the block, to the 174th Street corner, and turned the corner, and stopped in front of the black door of a boarded-up storefront. There was a big, Gothic F painted on it in silver, with a peephole stuck in the curves between the fancy horizontal strokes. Bill rang the bell, then knocked in the secret code. It began to feel very mysterious and great to me, like a secret society, something the Bullets never thought of having. A girl opened the door, and Bill signaled me to follow him in. It was beautiful inside, I mean for just some kids to have a place like this of their own. There were some old rugs on the floor, and some easy chairs and a couch where the girl who had opened the door sat down. Maybe the Fanwoods weren't so stupid. There was even a big round kitchen table, and a refrigerator, an old one with the motor on top, and a big electric hot plate on a shelf. The Bullets were new, and that was our excuse for not being comfortable, and the Fanwoods had been around for years, from before World War II. So they had a clubhouse, a pad. There was a big Knickerbocker Beer sign on the wall that lit up, with a clock in the middle, and a giant fight poster of Billy Conn, the Irish boxer, who almost beat Joe Louis before the war, but got too cocky and threw his face against one of Louis' rights in the thirteenth round and was put to sleep. He fought him again after the war, but Conn had lost his cockiness by then and his machine guns just sputtered against Louis' amazing cannons right and left. Another poster, which I couldn't believe, was of the full furry head of Albert Einstein. How did he get into the Fanwoods' clubhouse? He looked almost stupid staring across the room at Billy Conn. It was a weird neighborhood, in a weird world.

"You're lucky to get to see this place," said Bill, obviously proud of the room. "Most of the Fanwoods never get to see it." He explained that the premises were reserved for the use of Ryan and his lieutenants, and an occasional limited war conference before a rumble. Sometimes they'd let in a younger Fanwood who'd got his lumps in a fight, and needed something to make him feel good. "And we let girls in," he whispered in my ear, "If they put out." I looked down at the girl on the couch, and she stared right into my eyes. She looked like any other girl, popping her Bazooka bubble gum, but it was a shock looking into the eyes of a girl who put out. She was not really pretty, but she was neatly dressed. She looked nice. Maybe she was sixteen. I couldn't believe she was someone who did it.

"You sit down over there," Bill pointed at a seat next to the girl. "But don't touch the merchandise." He disappeared into the back room.

I sat down and looked straight ahead, and felt the eyes of "the merchandise" looking right into my ear.

"I never saw you before. When did they let you in the Fanwoods?"

I'd forgotten I was wearing the black and silver jacket. "I'm not in the Fanwoods," I said.

"What? No," she said, and moved closer to me, as if to take a better look. Her body had a sour smell, like she'd been sweating, and I wondered if she'd just done it. She wore a green plaid skirt, and a white blouse, and a blue sweater, and she had little gold wires through her ears. I stared at them. I'd never seen a girl with pierced ears before. She caught me looking at them, and reached up and touched her ear and smiled. That made me feel peculiar.

"How come you're not a Fanwood?" she asked.

"I'm a Bullet," I said. "I'm wearing Kevin's jacket." I hoped that would keep her from moving closer to me. I was afraid she could have been a nympho in that room. Some girls were nymphos, like Abigail Musselman. I hadn't yet met her so I didn't know, but I did know that they were never satisfied. They swallowed men like egg creams.

"Whose jacket?" she said, leaning towards me.

"Big Kevin," I said, bending away from her. She seemed nice enough, like a lot of other girls, but it was dark in that room, one little floor lamp lit, and I didn't want her to grab me, because if she started I wouldn't be able to hold back, because once a boy gets hot he's not a thinking person any more, he's an animal. He acts like a dog. And what I feared at that time

was that the Fanwoods could have her trained. She would get
me hot, and doing it, and then she'd clamp up. Then all the
Fanwoods would come in. Or maybe they'd call some cops, and
I'd be caught. Statutory rape.

"What's a Bullet?" she asked.

Either she was stupid, or she was playing with me. I moved
to the edge of the couch and leaned over as if to tie my
sneaker, but I was wearing my loafers. I took the penny out of
the slot and read the date. It wasn't a 1909S VDB, which was
worth a lot of money. It was 1936, the year I was born.

"Don't you hear good?" she asked.

"What? Why?"

"I asked what's a Bullet."

"It's a club, like the Fanwoods, only we've got purple and
gold."

"But that's the Fanwood jacket," she said, actually reaching
out to touch the one I wore.

I smiled at her. "There's a story behind it."

She sat up straight and smiled herself. She looked cute. "I
don't believe you're a Bullet." That was an oblique compliment.
She took her Bazooka gum off her tongue, looked at it a
second, then popped it back in her mouth.

"What's your name?" I asked.

"Mary," she said. "Mary Ryan. I'm his sister." She pointed at
the door to the back room where Jack Ryan himself was standing and watching us. That was a shock. He started towards the
couch. I had thought Jack Ryan was some other kid I saw at
the schoolyard that day. This was the exact kid who had
punched me out in my courtyard.

"So you met my sister," he said. He gave her a little gesture
with his head, and she crossed the room to sit down in the

easy chair by the floor lamp under the Einstein picture, and pulled a copy of the *Police Gazette* into her lap. Jack Ryan sat down on the couch next to me. I was embarrassed by the thoughts I'd had about his sister.

"Does your sister stay here all the time?"

"Hey. Forget my sister."

"I just ..."

"Leave her alone."

That was my mistake, a stupid way to start talking about the Bullets and the Fanwoods. I kept quiet for a minute and looked at Ryan. He looked older than fifteen, the way his face wrinkled up when he talked. I was sure he didn't recognize me as the kid he had punched out once. That didn't mean much to him, just punching a kid once. I had never punched anyone, so for me that could have been important.

"So we're gonna rumble," he said. "The Bullets and the Fanwoods. Nice."

I realized that kid, Bill, had told him that was why I was here. "No. No." I said. "We don't want to fight. I came to talk about that. We're not fighters."

Ryan shot up from his seat and started pacing around the room. I felt something very dangerous about him. He scared me, but I was fascinated too. I had never been with anyone like this before. It was like being in a cage with a leopard. I had no idea what he was going to do next. I mean, he could have served me up for dinner, no problem. He pulled the magazine off his sister's lap, looked at, and threw it back down. Then he came back to the couch and looked at me like no one had ever looked at me before. I'd never seen blue eyes burn like that before—a mean, ruthless fire, a guy whose nerves were always burning, who never stopped moving inside. That was why he looked so much older. He grabbed me by that Fanwood jacket and picked me off the couch like I weighed a small ounce.

"Look, faggot, the only reason you came in here, the only reason we let you in here, is to figure when and where we're gonna rumble. We don't let anyone in here. So you can choose the battleground. If you say chains, we bring chains. If you say knuckles, we bring our brass. We don't fight with knives or zip guns. That's for spics. Now you know why you're in here. That's all." He let me drop back onto the couch. This was embarrassing in front of his sister. I was in a very stupid position, and in front of a girl, though she didn't seem to be paying any attention to it. She was chewing her gum and reading the magazine, like this was what happened every day.

"I came here by myself," I said. "I can't say I represent all the Bullets." He looked as if he didn't even hear that. I suddenly wondered why I had come here at all. What good could it do? It looked now like if anything I would screw things up. I had nothing to bargain with. I mean, in the Fanwoods' terms, the Bullets had no power. A rumble with us for them would be like mopping the floor. We weren't the Condors. I shouldn't have done this without talking to the rest of the guys, even though I believe that reasonable is reasonable. Peaceful means. Negotiations, I believed in. But I also realized that you've got to hold some power in the face of violence, otherwise talk was empty words. I would have liked a conference with little Gandhi just at that point. How did he do it? By himself.

"You don't look bad in a Fanwood jacket," Ryan said, playing with me a little. "What's your name?"

"I'm Swanson. Bill Swanson."

"That's not a Jew name."

I looked at his sister, and then the picture above her head. "My name is Einstein," I said.

"O yeah. I throw darts at that picture. E equals MC squared. What do you know about that?"

"Nothing," I said. "My mother is Jewish, and my father is Irish," I said.

"That's the theory of relativity. And your mother is a who-er." His sister looked up from her magazine at the word.

"I want to talk to you about your mother. She's a who-er. You don't want to talk about a rumble, I'm gonna talk about your mother. She's a who-er. All the Fanwoods fucked her."

That was supposed to get me pissed and, of course, it did. Somewhere inside of me there was always my Irish that got hot. I kept my eye on Einstein, however, and that kept me cool. What kind of Fanwood was Einstein?

"Every one of us fucked your mother, one night." Ryan looked at his sister who pretended again not to be listening. He liked to make me seem wimpy in front of her. He would have loved me to jump him right there, an excuse for him to smash me up by himself and serve my remains out the door of the clubhouse to his hungry black and silver horde. Maybe he could have done that, I thought, but I would have got a piece of him that he would have missed for life, just like my father said. I hated those thoughts, but they were born in me, and luckily I was also born chicken enough not to act on my Irish. Like I said, I think too much, and I bruise too easy.

"I came here," I said after a moment, "to talk about Florry O'Neill, and Fred Sugarman. To see if we could have peace, not to arrange a rumble."

"Florry O'Neill, huh?" A bunch of wrinkles clouded his face.

"She's a who-er too." His voice had a peculiar high-pitched whine.

"She's my friend," his sister piped up.

"Shut up, Mary," Ryan said in his squeakier voice. He walked over to her and pointed at the door of the clubhouse. She gave him a dirty look, smiled at me, and left.

"You forget about my sister," he said. "And you take that Fanwood jacket off." He grabbed it out of my hand and took it to the back room, and told Bill to take it over to Kevin, and to get my jacket back. Then he came back to the couch.

"You think I care about Florry O'Neill? I don't care about Florry O'Neill. She's a fucking bitch, and she deserves to go down with the Bullets. With what's his name? Why didn't that Jew prick come here?"

"It was my idea. I came here on my own."

These guys were a world different from the Bullets. They had organization. They were an old gang. There were some of them even twenty-two now, some guys in the army in Korea, who once were Fanwoods. By comparison the Bullets were just made up one afternoon. We had the weakness of individuals.

"He didn't come because he knew I'd kill him if I saw him," Ryan grinned his meanest.

"I thought you didn't care about Florry O'Neill."

He slapped my face. "Fuck your mother."

I rubbed my cheek. Funny that it didn't hurt. I would have loved to say some tough sure line, like Bogart. "You'll regret that some day." But I didn't have the mind or the heart to do it.

"I don't care about her. You can tell Fred Whatzisname that he can have Florry O'Neill. I don't need her. She put out for me. She put out for all the Fanwoods. Tell him that. Florry O'Neill put out for all the Fanwoods one night."

Bill came back with my jacket. Ryan took it from him, and threw it at me. "She wants to wear one of these pieces of shit, she can wear it."

"If you don't care about her, why do you want to fight the Bullets? Why can't we just ignore everything, be friendly."

"We're not friendly with faggots. We're the Fanwoods. We've got our friends, and this is where we are."

I put on my jacket. The time was coming to leave, and it was a touchy time, to get out of there in one piece.

"Look, punk," he said. "I could kill you right now, and no one would ever find your pieces. I can do what I want." That sounded weird, for someone to say that. I had never heard anyone say he could kill me before, except the atom bomb, that says it every second. Did he mean it? It almost sounded like he'd do me a favor. "And I'll tell you some more, it ain't Florry O'Neill. There's a lot of girls around here. Shit. Florry O'Neill. It's not her. The reason we're after the Bullets is because we hate the Bullets. We hate," and he pushed his face close to mine, "the faggot Jew Bullets, and that's why we're going to stomp you. That's why. And I'll tell you that you'll be okay now, maybe, but you come around here again and you'll be dead." He pulled his hand across his throat like a blade. "Dead."

I could have put my tail between my legs and left right at that point but I didn't. I waited to get something else in. "Hey, look, Ryan, I came here, and I didn't know what was going to happen. I could be dead now, right. We don't like to fight. We don't like to get hurt, and we don't want to hurt anybody."

"Who you gonna hurt, Bullet?" I wished I could grin like him, so evil.

"You guys like to fight so much, Ryan, who don't you go to Korea? General MacArthur needs you over there."

"You telling me where to go fight? The Bullets are just chicken."

I had him just a little off balance, and it was fun, though if I wasn't careful I could be carried home on a stretcher. "It's just stupid to fight over something like this, over a girl. If you're gonna fight, fight a war. Fight for democracy. Go to Korea." It sounded stupid even to me. Who wanted to go to Korea and fight over there? In fact, that was more stupid than fighting over Florry O'Neill. Who understood Korea? I was just making it up, trying to talk my way out of something for myself, for my friends. It was words.

"Purple and gold chicken feathers. That's what it is. Chicken Bullets."

"Look," I said. "I've got this great idea. Instead of fighting why don't we play a game?"

"Get out of here." He pushed me towards the door.

"We can play basketball. Bullets against the Fanwoods. Or if you wait till next spring we can play hardball."

"Get out of here, punk." He pushed me through the door.

"We're gonna play the Condors next spring. Hardball." Sometimes I want to congratulate myself on how I can time a lie. This was a gift, maybe, from my father.

"You're going to play the Condors?" He couldn't believe that.

"We're gonna play. The game is scheduled already, next May 14, at Dyckman Street. We already reserved the field."

"Fuckin' Condors." I was on one side of the door now and he was on the other. "Look Swanson, don't let me catch you around here again, or any of your Bullets. I don't play games, and we're not going to play baseball with the Bullets. We're gonna look for you on the streets. We're gonna find you at school. We'll find you, Swanson, and we'll stomp your ass. We'll stomp you one at a time till you rumble with us, because that's how we see it." Having said that he smiled, almost nicely, as he was closing the door. "I like you, Swanson," he said. "You could be a Fanwood." Ryan shut the door and I stood there staring at the big Gothic F, his last words buzzing in my ears. I could be a Fanwood. I could just as easily be a nun. But he was right. With a name like Swanson I could be a Fanwood. It's a question of where you live. I live on the other side of Broadway, and that's why I'm a Bullet. It's like North and South Korea. But I also knew that even if I lived here, near St. Nich or Amsterdam, even then I couldn't be a Fanwood; not in my heart, which was a peaceful heart, like the heart of Mahatma Gandhi.

What do they get out of it? I never understood it. I mean, even in New York City you can watch the Hudson River flow under the George Washington Bridge, and you can watch it forever, and your heart can feel big, and that's in the middle of the city. Why does anyone want to hurt someone else? I'll never understand it; I mean, I'm more used to it now. If you've survived in our century, our hypocritical pimping whoremaster rabid bitch of a century, you have to have witnessed personally on TV all kinds of murders, dismemberments, random massacres, institutionalized genocide, planned apathy of vested interests in political terror—the ongoing rape of the poor people of the earth. You have to have seen your own country condone, in fact, instigate it. You have to have seen Henry Kissinger, from your own neighborhood, rationalize policies that mean misery and death for thousands of poor people. But not just Kissinger, the poor faggot of a lost intellectual, living in a hell he chose, half blind himself to his own life. You know once I saw him in the house where he lived up on 52nd Street. I was visiting a potential client there, a rich guy who owned an apartment in the same building, and when I walked in the doormen muscled me into a corner because Kissinger was coming out to his limousine. He had six bodyguards. It was like a Kissinger sandwich—three big guys in front of him and three in back, all of them moving together with short steps. What idiot would choose to live that way?

"Hey, Henry," I shouted. I couldn't resist. "The Fanwoods are coming."

One of the doormen leaned against me. "You crazy, buddy?" he said, his accent Greek or Arab or something.

"No," I said. "I'm a Bullet." Kissinger drove away in his bulletproof limo. I walked down the hall in my Florsheim shoes.

And now the madness of our weapons. You can see I go crazy if I even begin to think about it. It's like these habits of violence make us stand here now with these sledgehammers in our hands waiting to smash ourselves over the head. I mean what planet do those guys advocating nuclear buildup think they live on?

Washington Heights. O Christ, O Jesus, I thought, standing outside the door of the Fanwoods' clubhouse. This is where I live. I looked up and down 174th Street. There were no black jackets in sight, and it was really peaceful. A woman came down the stairs with a big Doberman on a leash. I don't have anything against Dobermans, but I don't think of one as a dog. They look at you and you feel like a piece of meat. I don't even think Doberman puppies are cute. This Doberman looked at me, and the woman started walking my way with it. This Doberman had a spiked collar on. It was not a peaceful dog. I stepped back into the Fanwoods' doorway as they passed, and then, as if I was shot from a gun, I took off across 174th Street towards St. Nich. Near the corner a girl was sitting by herself on a stoop. She stood up as I got close to her. It was Mary Ryan.

"Hi," she said.

"O, hi," I said, and looked around. It wouldn't be exactly comfortable for me to be seen with her on the street.

"Look, I knew you were a Bullet. I knew everything," she said. "Florry O'Neill is my best friend. She likes the Bullets."

"Good," I said. Then I smiled because it seemed funny. "That's what the problem is, isn't it?"

She walked beside me towards Broadway. "I don't like the way my brother treated you. The Bullets are nice. Florry told me about it. But Jack, you know...he's got some problems."

"Yeah," I said.

"I think you're a nice guy. I think it's real good that you came to talk to him."

"It didn't do any good."

"You never know. Jack isn't as bad as he seems. It's good that he just met you. Someone like you. You know he really reads all about Albert Einstein."

"What for? Einstein is Jewish."

"Jack don't care about all that. Jack is smart. He always wants to learn something. He's just crazy too."

"Good," I said. I wanted to get away from her. Any minute some black and silver jackets could show up and see us talking alone. Sugarman and Florry O'Neill were enough.

"Look," I said. "We're giving a game and dance at the Y next week, on 178th Street. Why don't you come. Girls are free."

"Gee, thanks, I'm sure, Swanny." She looked at me as if I'd told her something absolutely wonderful. She looked at me as if she liked me, and at that time, under those conditions, that was frightening.

"I'll see you later," I said, and I crossed over Broadway, and I thought, holy shit, what did I tell her. At one point while I was talking to Jack Ryan I thought about inviting him and the Fanwoods to the dance, just for a second I thought of it, but then I thought again. That would have been crazy. This was even crazier. Now I invited his sister. This could start a war. This was like bombing Pearl Harbor. I should never have gone there, I should have stayed on my side of Broadway. I turned around when I got across, and she was still standing there near the gas station. She waved at me, and I waved back. Mother Macree, I thought, and oy vey. I slipped into Zooky's for the comfort of an egg cream.

"Okay. I'll do it," said Zooky, as soon as he saw me.

"What?"

"I've been thinking about it. Zooky's will sponsor the Bullets."

"Oh yeah," I said. "That's good, Zooky. I need a vanilla egg cream."

"On the house," he said, something he could never do if his wife were in the store. "You know we never had any kids."

"That's too bad," I said. "Kids are nice."

"Yeah, and the Bullets are nice kids," he said. "I want your uniforms to say *Zooky's Newsstand and Confectionery*. I like confectionery better than candystore."

"Sure," I said.

"I even like the name. The Bullets. It's a strong name."

I looked at Zooky, his eyes swimming behind his thick glasses like fish in a bowl. My hand was trembling with the egg cream in it. I got it to my mouth. It tasted almost too sweet. I swallowed it down quickly, and I went home.

You could have been in Germany sometimes when you walked into the old YM and YWHA where we held our games and dances. Not a word of English in the place, just some old German Jewish ladies jabbering in Deutsch in the lounge, their silent old husbands sitting in the easy chairs reading the *Aufbau* and smoking cigars, whose smoke created a horrible smell to walk through before you played ball; but when those women were in the kitchen, baking for their "kaffeeklatsch" the air would smell so sweet and buttery you'd get fat just walking to the gym. And the way these old German people looked at you they made you feel like you came through the wrong door to pick up the garbage, or maybe that you were the garbage walking in the door. It was like the "Fourth Reich" in there.

The place had an old smell, like I imagined the attics must smell of people who live in small towns. No attics in Washington Heights. The old board floors were full of dust, paint peeling off the gray walls, green doors everywhere with textured glass rattling in them, old couches and easy chairs with upholstery worn to the threads. A portrait of Chaim Weitzman hung above the big couch in the lounge, and all around the rooms someone had gone crazy framing Norman Rockwell *Saturday Evening Post* covers, though some people complained he was a famous antisemite. The kids in his pictures sure looked more like Fanwoods than like Bullets.

This was a tired old beige brick building that complained when you walked through it, and if you jumped it seemed to threaten collapse. It's a good thing the gym was in the basement, and the dances were held there and not in the upstairs auditorium. The place was ready to die on its own, and we all felt it. But it still hit like a tragedy when it was finally torn down, because for many of the kids in the neighborhood everything that happened in their lives actually took off from there. The Hebrew School was there. The neighborhood day camp was organized and took off from there in the summer, and the arts and crafts continued there in the winter. You learned to dance there, and got your first crush there; and, of course, you got to play basketball there in a gym in a league with a referee and a trophy.

It was a firetrap. Everyone said it; in fact, it was condemned, was going to be torn down to make way for the Port Authority bus station that sits on that spot now, but it was rescued for this one last year. We didn't realize how much we'd miss it until it was gone. When they finally swung the wrecker's ball at its old walls, and we saw it give in so willingly, relax and embrace the ball when it hit, and then when we saw the empty space, it was like someone had died, an accommodating old aunt we'd all loved, eccentric, but open to us, whom we had taken for granted, but who we suddenly understood could never be replaced.

Before our game we didn't know anything about the Royals, except what Baldeen had told us, and I don't want to cast aspersions on the Bronx—a borough in which, at the time, I had several aunts and uncles on my mother's side living quite happily; but at first it looked like these guys from up on the Grand Concourse had come to Manhattan with the intention of doing the fake-out of the year. It took them two subways and a bus to get to us, so I grant they were serious about playing, but when I saw them at first I didn't believe it. They had brought what looked like the great ringer with them, a black guy who must have been six foot three. This was long before blacks dominated professional basketball. Everyone knew the Harlem Globetrotters, but they were a bunch of clowns working for Al Saperstein—negroes, as polite liberal white people, who weren't prejudiced, still called them. Everyone's heroes in basketball were like George Mikan, the biggest white man on earth; Bob Cousy, who culd do anything with a basketball; Ernie Vandeweghe; Carl Braun on the Knicks, with his one-hander; 'Tricky Dick McGuire'; Easy Ed Macauley, who looked like you could break him in pieces he was so tall and frail and white, like all the rest. It was just before the era of Elgin Baylor and Oscar Robertson, before Wilt Chamberlain and Bill Russel. It was a white game, more businesslike, slower strategies, almost totally on the floor. The two-hand set shot was still a shot. The blacks came in, not like they did in baseball, with the big publicity like for Jackie Robinson; but they eased in quietly through the colleges, and they made the game more beautiful—turned it into a gorgeous aerobatic dance— and even today most white roundball players play as if they're doing business—less flash, more of the job to be done—and blacks play out some choreography of escape from economic slavery. I mean, they take risks; I mean, they survive on the basketball court, with all the flamboyance that follows their success.

We all stood on the steps down to the gym and the locker room and watched this black guy come down, like he'd just got in from outer space. Grossman looked like his eyes were ready to jump out of his face and bounce around on the floor. "Ungawa," Dufner said, as the guy passed him. I think it was the first time a black guy was ever in that Y, no less in the locker room to play a game, and if we were there feeling weird about it I could imagine how he must have been feeling.

"I ain't gonna play with a nigger," Dufner said. He was really dressed to cha-cha-cha: lime-green pegged pants with saddle stitching; a one-button, single breasted, pale blue cardigan jacket; a bright yellow shirt with the long collar; and to top it off at the bottom he had on a pair of blue suede shoes. All the money he ever made from all his little scams went into cool clothes. A little darker complexion and he would have looked fine himself on the corner of Amsterdam and 125th Street.

"What's the difference," Zoo said. "You like jazz."

"I don't like jazz. I never liked jazz."

"Why'd you sneak into Birdland with us once?"

"That doesn't mean I like jazz. I like to sneak, but I don't have to like jazz."

"You snuck into the Palladium too."

"That's Puerto Rican. That's Spanish music."

"What's the difference? Some of them are black."

"Tell that to a spic and see. They speak Spanish, that's the difference. Look, what is this? The Inquisition? I just don't want to play with a nigger. You guys play." He smoothed down his jacket and shirt collar. His real reason, I think, was that he didn't want to strip to play basketball, and not that he had anything against this black guy.

"They're just as good as we are," Zoo said.

"Speak for yourself. I don't want to be in the locker room with them. If you want to take the same shower, that's up to you."

"You're just afraid to lose," Grossman said. "You're afraid he's too tall."

"I hope your sister marries one," Dufner said.

"I wouldn't care if my sister married one, if he was smart," Grossman said.

"Your sister...." Dufner started one of his famous attacks, but stopped, because he didn't want to risk messing up his clothes.

"Okay," said Sugarman, "Enough. Hubby'll cover the big guy. We'll put him on Stames' shoulders."

That didn't cheer us up much. It took us forever to get our clothes off, and get into our sneakers and shorts. It was our game and dance and we were faked out before it even began. We didn't stand a whisper of a chance against the giant of the world. It didn't even seem worth the effort to undress.

The kid's name was Roland, and it turned out he actually was on the Royals, went to Bronx Science with some of them. His father was a lawyer, the family actually from Abyssinia, escaped Mussolini's henchmen to come to the U.S., and to top it off, they were Jewish. How do you figure that?

I was glad that no one ever came to watch the games. It was bad enough that at the dance some girl might ask you how the game came out and you'd have to tell her you lost. The game started around five o'clock when everyone was eating dinner anyway, and the dance didn't start till after eight usually, so you missed the game unless you were a special girlfriend, like Florry, who came for a little of the first half, but disappeared, happily, before halftime. I say "happily" because in the second half we were slaughtered.

There was one guy, though, who did show up to watch all the games. He was a fat, greasy guy, a little weird, who we called Onions. What can I say? He called himself Onions. His breath—if you wanted to get close enough to him to smell it, which sometimes across the room was close enough—always smelled like onions. He must have been forty years old. I knew him because he washed pots and mopped the floors on weekends at Deuce Douros' father's restaurant. If there was a queer in the neighborhood, it was Onions. He'd bring a bag full of sandwiches and pickles and french fries and candy bars and a quart of milk, and he'd sit on the sidelines watching the boys play ball and stuff his mouth. Onions wasn't just weird, he was retarded. I doubt that he even knew himself that he liked boys. He'd stay till the end, watching us run up and down the court, and then he'd leave before the dance.

The first half of the game we didn't do too bad. Roland, it turned out, was real clumsy. Stames, who played center for us, and wasn't your great example of finesse, had no trouble faking this kid out just by lifting his shoulder. Once Stames just lifted an arm and the kid began to jump around like a spastic, and then he fell down, and so Stames turned around and put in an easy lay-up. If Roland grabbed a rebound by mistake, whoever was standing next to him, whether a Bullet or a Royal, could just take the ball out of his hands like it was a gift. He might as well have been four foot six, not six foot three. It wasn't Roland who gave us the trouble. It was a little kid they called Coony, who I was covering.

We passed the ball good in the first half, and spread out their zone, and Schletzbaum hit a couple of long set-shots, and Stames scored a couple of baskets, when Roland stumbled, and I drove to the basket a few times. One shot I was proud of I made going up in the air from the right side of the basket, and floating underneath and spinning to put it in off the backboard from the left. I don't know how I did it, and I don't know how I looked, and I never did it again, but I still remember making that shot. Even now getting older I can still feel it in my body. With about eight seconds to go in the half they were ahead 18-16, and Sugarman hit me with a pass near half court, and I dribbled a couple of times, and everyone was shouting "Shoot! Shoot!" and so I threw the ball up. I couldn't even see the basket from half court. It was like the wind was in my eyes, but the ball went in, swish, hardly rippling the cords.

"What ass. What ass. You shot that ball with your ass, Swanny," they all shouted at me as we floated into the locker room, the game tied up 18-18.

"The bazooka," said Zoo.

"Ass and a half," said Schletzbaum.

They were right. I didn't shoot that ball. I just threw it up into the airs of fate. I wish I could open up and do that some more now in my life—just throw it up and let it blow. More ass, less thought.

Mr. Press—who out of the goodness of his heart and real interest in the kids would officiate these games and chaperone the dances with his wife—congratulated me on my shots. Kutzer sometimes showed up too, but no one ever asked him to be a referee. If he ever made a call it would always be the wrong call. So we felt great at halftime. The second half was going to be a romp. Everything would go in the basket. I had the image of myself as Tricky Dick McGuire, playmaker, in the second half, passes behind the back, dribbling between the legs, going up and laying it off to Stames in the lane. Two points every time.

The second half opened with a shot by Schletzbaum, trying to beat my half-court shot. It was an air ball, went completely out of bounds, nowhere near the backboard. After that the Royals began to roll out of sight. Coony, who I was guarding, hadn't taken any shots at all in the first half, just drove around me once and scored when I went for the ball and missed; but in the second half he started gunning, and I couldn't believe it. I was guarding him, and I had two inches on him, and I was quick and played pretty good defense, but I had no idea at all of how to stop his shot. I let him take the first one, because it was from about fifteen feet, and I figured if it went in it was luck. Swish. The second one I stayed closer to him. He was fast, but I didn't have any trouble keeping up. I thought I threw a hand up in his face when he tried to take the shot, but my hand ended up nowhere near his face. This one spun around the rim and out. Coony did something that I had never seen before. He went up in the air to take his one-hander. They hadn't even started to do that in the pros yet. Carl Braun, who had the great one hander for the Knicks, took it from the floor. This kid had developed the jump shot all by himself, a compensation for being short.

I'd be right on top of him, hawking the ball all the way, and he'd dribble to the corner or to the top of the key, and take one step in and then suddenly a step back, and he'd be up in the air before I knew where he was, and swish. He took about ten shots in the second half, and made six of them, all off of me. It was terrifying. There was nothing I could do. It even froze me up on offense. I didn't drive to the bucket once in the whole second half. I just stood at the right side of the key and acted like a turnstile; the ball came to me and I passed it off. I was in shock. The Royals beat us by twelve points, those twelve points scored against me by Coony. I felt horrible at the end. I felt like Onions, who dragged out of the gym as soon as the game was over, holding his brown bag upside down so his garbage dribbled to the floor as he crossed the court. I sat by myself in a corner of the locker room and didn't even take a shower for a long time. Roland came over and sat down with me. His legs took up so much of his body I was almost as tall as he was sitting down.

"You guys played a good game," he said.

"Yeah, we stunk; especially me."

"It was just Coony who beat you," he said. "You probably would have won if we didn't have Coony. He's a ringer. He plays for Clinton."

"He's in high school?" He was so small he looked like the youngest guy on the team.

"Yeah, and if he was my size I bet he could be a pro. I stink at sports."

"You played good."

"It's a good thing I like science," he said.

"You could play ball too."

"I met Dr. Drew once, Dr. Charles Drew. You heard of him?"

"Uh uh."

"See, that's what I mean. He invented the method of storing blood plasma. Saved a lot of people's lives. He died this year in North Carolina, on April first, in a car accident."

"That's too bad," I said. He was looking at me in this special way, so I knew he wanted to get the most out of this story he was telling.

"He was nice man. He knew my father, and he told me I should come to see him when I want to go to medical school. His car smashed up in North Carolina, and he died because they wouldn't let him into a 'whites only' hospital for a blood transfusion, and he lost too much blood."

"Really?"

"Some April Fool's joke."

I didn't know where to look. Roland had this grin on his face so I couldn't tell which was more important, that he felt sad about the death, or that he got to tell me the story. He kept looking at me. Maybe he wanted me to apologize, to suffer, for what happened to Dr. Drew.

"It sounds like what happened to Bessie Smith," I finally said.

"Yeah." He paused. "Who's Bessie Smith?"

I couldn't believe it, but I didn't dare say "she's one of your people." "She's the greatest blues singer of all time. Sometimes Symphony Sid will play her old records. She died on the steps of a white hospital."

"We don't listen to that stuff much at home. My mom plays the cello and my dad messes with the piano. They like Mozart."

The Royals didn't stay for the dance. They had a long trip back to the Bronx. I felt a little better knowing Coony was the ringer on a high school team. I didn't do too bad against him. In a year or two I'd stop his jump shot. No problem.

Dufner was on his tiptoes on a ladder when we got back to the gym, covering the grates of the lights with pink paper.

"You want it a little pink in here," he shouted down. "The pink atmosphere. It gets them hot. You don't want too much blue."

"Where's Douros?" Sugarman asked.

"He'll get here," I said. "He's only playing from eight to ten, two hours."

"By the time he sets up," Sugarman said, "it'll be eight-thirty."

"So he'll play till eleven," I said. "No problem."

"We've got to be out of here by eleven." Sugarman threw his arms up in the air like a mad organizer.

"Relax, Sugarman," I said. I could tell that he wasn't really worried, but wanted to look like everything depended on him, to impress Florry who was sitting on a bench in a corner, never taking her eyes off him. There was another girl with her, who kept smiling at me. I smiled back, but it took me a long time to recognize who she was. Mary Ryan. Jack Ryan's sister. She looked totally different, dressed in a plaid skirt, and a blouse, her dark hair hanging down. She almost looked grown-up.

"Oh Christ, she's here," I thought out loud. I mean, I wasn't exactly glad to see her.

"Who's here?" asked Schletzbaum, who was holding the ladder for Dufner, and had overheard me.

"We've had it," I said, and I grabbed Schletzbaum. "Did you tell your father?"

"Tell my father what?"

"Hold the ladder," Dufner shouted. "If I fall off and get blood on my clothes you pay the cleaning bills."

"Blood won't come off," Schletzbaum shouted back. "Tell my father what?"

"Shit," said Dufner, as the roll of scotch tape slipped to the floor.

"Am I the only one who thinks about it? Tell him that we were having this dance and that it's possible, even likely, that the Fanwoods are going to come to bust it up."

"He said to call him if there's any trouble."

"I don't want cops. Cops are not sexy," Dufner said.

"This isn't a joke. By the time we call him. . . ."

"Listen, my father's got gambling, rape, murder, all in this nice neighborhood. He hasn't got time for some kids."

"We need atmosphere, Swanny. We don't need cops. Cops are not pink," Dufner said.

"Very funny," I said.

"Cops are not atmosphere. It's pink, and you dance close. Abigail Musselman is going to be here. The only cop you need is to cop a feel."

"Fuck a feel. I didn't come here to cop a feel."

"What did you come for? To fight with the Fanwoods?" Dufner grabbed the scotch tape and headed back up the ladder. "There are no Fanwoods. Fanwoods are not pink. No Fanwoods tonight."

They had my head spinning. Was I making it up? Was this only my fight? Was this all going on only in my Irish-Jewish head?

"You look real sharp up there, Dufner," said Grossman, passing by. "Sharp as a matzo."

"And twice as crummy," said Grossman and Schletzbaum and Dufner himself, in unison.

"Schletzbaum, do you see that girl over there sitting with Sugarman's Florry?"

Schletzbaum looked at me as if I was the greatest pain in the ass in the world. "Which girl?" I turned his head to demonstrate for him the only two girls so far in the room, sitting together in the corner.

"That girl. With Florry. She's Mary Ryan. That's Jack Ryan's sister."

"So? Do you like her?"

"You're being stupid, Schletzbaum. You're being a schmuck, on purpose. It isn't whether I like her or not. I don't like girls, okay. But what if Jack Ryan knows she's here? What if he sent her here on purpose? It's his sister."

"So she'll beat us all up. What are you telling me? This is a dance."

"Cha-cha-cha." Dufner jumped off the ladder.

"Look, okay," said Schletzbaum. "My father's on duty tonight. If the Fanwoods come I'll call. He'll have a squad car here in five minutes."

"Five minutes," I said, a heavy note of fatality in my voice.

"Swanny, relax," Schletzbaum said.

"Somebody come here and hold the ladder," Dufner shouted from the next light.

"Just enjoy the dance, Swanny. There'll be lots of girls here. Ryan's sister is pretty. Look, we'll all die together."

He was right, and I realized it. I was exaggerating the danger; maybe because I thought I'd lost the game single-handedly I expected disaster to follow on disaster.

"Hey, Dufner," Stames shouted up at him. "This is a gym. No matter what you do to it, it'll never be Roseland. It's still gonna smell like basketball."

"Where's the damned band?" Sugarman shouted. "Where is Deuce Douros and the fucking Aces?"

"They're at music school," Dufner shouted down. "Learning to play 'Blue Moon'."

Florry came over and threw her arms around Sugarman's neck and hung onto his back. She looked pretty in a white cotton dress with petticoats and pink bobby socks. She had pale skin, some light freckles on her nose, and light pink lipstick. She looked real feminine and nice. Mary Ryan stood watching her hang like a white kitten from Sugarman's back as he swung her from side to side. Mary kept looking at me, and I kept looking away. I felt stupid for not talking to her, but all I needed, I thought, was Mary Ryan swinging on my back.

She did seem different out of the Fanwood territory, a lot softer, though it seemed to me anyone would soften up in the whisper of Florry O'Neill's pretty light.

"Don't worry," I said, finally moving up next to her. "The dance'll start soon."

"Do you remember me?"

"Sure."

"I bet you didn't think I'd come."

"I was wondering," I said. "Do you think your brother'll come?"

"I didn't tell him about it. I don't talk to him much."

I saw Deuce Douros standing at the door in his slouched beret and shades. "Hey, Deuce. Gimme five," I shouted, then I said to Mary, my voice slipping into its cool tone, "Well if he does come, tell him I'm not going to dance with him."

"You're crazy," she laughed. "Later," I said. "Much later." The last under my breath as I left her for Deuce, who was holding something wrapped in velvet in his arms like a baby.

"This is my new Zildjian, man. Wait till you hear it." He pulled back the velvet to show me the brass. "Grab my bass drum. It's at the top of the stairs."

A girl stood at the head of the stairs next to Deuce's drums. From her long blonde hair and black dress you could tell she wanted to look like June Christy, but her body tended to Kate Smith.

"Who are you?" she asked, when I grabbed the handle of the drum case.

"I'm Swanny," I said.

"I'm Sylvia Tweet." She made it sound more like "twit." "I sing with the band."

"Gee, I thought you were June Christy," I said.

"Yeah, and I thought you were Stan Kenton."

I grabbed the handle of the bass drum case.

"Deuce told me not to let anyone touch his drums."

"I'm his friend," I said, heading down the stairs.

"Hey, you like June Christy?" she said.

"I like Anita O'Day," I said. "Sometimes she sounds like Billie Holiday; I like Billie. But I hate Dinah Washington. She's too fat to sing." I felt bad about that as soon as I said it, because I meant it to be nasty. I used to do that a lot at the time, insult girls when I talked to them.

Deuce set up his new Zildjian cymbal first. He looked very cool in his shades and beret, like Dizzy Gillespie. He was just fifteen, but was already shaving, and with his slightly unhealthy, yellowish complexion he looked like he could be twenty-three. He tapped the cymbal and listened like a pro.

"You hear that?" he asked me. "O-rooney macvarteemo," he quoted Slim Gaillard. "Get the tom-tom and my snare, okay."

"I like Julie London. I like Sarah Vaughan, the divine one," I said to Sylvia still at the head of the stairs.

"Good for you," she said, coldly.

"Every night I listen to Symphony Sid. I stay up to listen to it. Do you sing 'Lullaby of Birdland'?"

"I didn't know it had words," she said.

"You'd sing it great, I'm sure. Ella Fitzgerald sings it." She followed me down the steps with the drums.

"You like Ella Fitzgerald, huh?"

"She's perfect. What can I say?"

The lights were dimmed now in the gym.

"Well," she said. "There are some fat singers that you like."

It was nice of her to give me a way out of my jerky remark.

"Fat doesn't make any difference, actually. Besides, I would call you zaftig, not fat. You're pleasingly plump."

"And you look like a string bean," she smiled. "I like string beans."

"Do you think it looks sexy in here?" I asked.

"It's pink. Pink looks stupid in a gym."

"You hear that, Dufner?" I shouted at him where he stood near the band. "She says pink looks stupid in a gym."

"Who's that, Sylvia Tweet? She looks stupid in a gym too. Did you bring your instrument?" Dufner asked.

"I sing," said Sylvia.

"Yeah, that's what I mean. Last time I saw you you forgot your voice. I sing too, in the shower." I started to push Dufner away from her.

"From the way you smell, I didn't think you ever took a shower," Sylvia said. She could handle herself.

"When you start to sing we'll turn the showers on," Dufner said. "Where are you pushing me?"

"There's a girl I think you should meet," I said.

"Hey, I'm a free American. I can walk. Don't push." Dufner smoothed out his clothes.

It was ten after eight. Kids were starting to show up at the door, and the band hadn't even finished setting up yet. They all stood looking in from the doorway as if they didn't know if it was the right place, or were afraid to come in.

"Your pink light has got them scared, Dufner."

"Up yours."

We walked up to Sugarman and Florry, who were smooching a little in the corner. Mary sat next to them, acting as if she didn't notice.

"Mary," I said. "I want you to meet somebody." I pulled

Frankie in from the shadows. "This is Frank Dufner. More than anyone else on the Bullets he is responsible for making all this happen." Sugarman heard the last sentence and pulled his face away from Florry's, and grinned. He thought I was talking about him.

"You know we don't have a chief, or a president of the Bullets, but if anyone is the kingpin, if you can point to anyone as indispensable and a driving force, it has to be Frank Dufner, right here."

"Bullshit," said Sugarman, then he looked at Florry, said "excuse me," and covered his mouth.

Dufner was beautiful, he was so stupid. He totally fell for it. He looked off into the pink lights like a boy of vision, for whom the future would not come soon enough. "I brought him here to meet you because I really thought you two would get along."

Sugarman was shaking his head. Mary stood up and smoothed down her skirt. "Frank Dufner," I said. "This is Mary Ryan."

"I'm glad to meet you," said Frank. "Thanks."

"She's the sister of Jack Ryan. You know Jack."

"Sure. Jack and I are old buddies. We were together in the war. He saved my life at the Anzio beachhead. Jack Ryan." He looked suddenly like something was dawning on him, and leaned over and whispered in my ear, "Jack Ryan?"

"Fanwoods," I whispered back.

Dufner stepped back and crossed his arms across his crotch, grinning as if he suddenly remembered he forgot to put on his pants. "Mary," he said. "Listen. I'm really glad to meet you, and I'd ask you to dance, but the band isn't playing yet. I'm going over to see if I can hurry them along. Maybe later I'll have some time to talk to you."

"Yeah, maybe you can walk her home, Frankie," I said.

Dufner looked at me, and said under his breath, "Prick," and then he left.

I turned back to Sugarman, who winked at me, approving finally my great fake-out. Mary looked confused, and I felt bad for a moment having had my joke at her expense.

"That was Dufner. He put the pink on all the lights."

"He sure looks sharp," she said.

"Yeah, sharp as a . . .," I hesitated, not knowing if these one-hundred percent Irish girls had ever seen a matzo.

"Sharp as a matzo, but twice as crummy," Florry grinned.

"Hey, you've really got her trained," I said to Sugarman.

"I'm a volunteer," said Florry. She was quick.

Finally the rest of the band arrived. It was Izzy Kaufman on piano, cockeyed Sidney Seligman on clarinet and saxophone, and they were supposed to have a bass, but he didn't show; Sylvia Tweet, of course, on vocals, and Deuce himself mashing the drums. They took forever to set up and get ready to play. Kids were filling the place up. Mr. Press and his wife, our chaperones, sat talking nicely in a corner. The girls accumulated on one side of the room, all ponytails and petticoats and poodle cuts and bobby socks. They sat, mostly, in twos and threes, their hands folded in their laps, bubbles growing here and there from the wads of Bazooka in their mouths. The guys on the other side swaggered around in bunches, laughing loudly, self-consciously, pushing each other into mock fights. Reuben Mamoulian came up and threw a hand in my face, and I blinked.

"Two for flinching," he said.

"C'mon Roobs," I said. I hated that stupid game.

"You flinched."

"Okay." I turned my left shoulder to him so he could have his two punches. If you were right-handed you gave your left shoulder. I didn't even feel the punches, because the person I saw coming in the door was Linda Cuebas. Her father had actually let her come. She was the prettiest in a light blue skirt printed with big flowers, puffed out with petticoats, and a lacy yellow blouse, and some high-heeled spike shoes, no bobby socks. She looked a lot older than thirteen and a half. That was why her father never let her out of his sight, why when I told her about the dance she said her father never let her go to dances. She was with her mother. They walked into the pink air, arm in arm. No matter what, I told myself, I was going to dance with her, even though I didn't know how to dance, even though I'd never danced before, I was going to do it with Linda Cuebas, at least a slow one or two. I knew I could do it.

It seemed forever, it always did, before the band was ready to play. They were infinitely fussy. Cockeyed Sidney Seligman sucked on his reeds as if he thought he was going to be Benny Goodman playing with the Philharmonic. Izzy Kaufman messed around inside the old upright as if he was figuring out how to invent the piano, and Deuce himself kept changing the position of his drums as if there was a certain nuance he could convey only with a certain special arrangement.

"Come on," said Dufner. "What are you doing? Writing the music?" Audrey Wolfe had arrived and stood with one hand on Dufner's shoulder, and one hand on her hip, looking at the band, smoking a cigarette. "Let's Cha-cha-cha," Dufner said and did a few steps around Audrey Wolfe. It seemed funny to me how Audrey Wolfe was older and yet tried to look even older than that.

Zoo had left after the game, and he came back now with his

date, who was Eva Hesse. I mentioned Henry Kissinger as the most famous kid to come out of our neighborhood, but may all the angels of Jayhood Wright Park knit sweaters of praise for Eva Hesse. She lived on 170th Street, which was as far south as any of the Bullets lived. I wouldn't ever have called her one of the Bullets' girls, but she did go out with Zoo on some dates. Eva Hesse became famous too, in her own way, and I don't even know if Zoo, who is now living in Indiana somewhere, I think, knows anything about it. I didn't know about it until one day I was in the Museum of Modern Art having lunch with a divorce client, sometimes girlfriend, who was a painter herself, and I saw the name of Eva Hesse on a placard on the wall. It impressed my friend that I could say I knew who she was, if it was the same Eva Hesse, which it was, because I saw her photo in the catalogue. The other artists had a bunch of stuff thrown on the floor, some string hanging from the wall, a mixmaster style pillow, a portrait of a bathrobe, and there in one corner with the name, Eva Hesse, were a bunch of things on the floor. They looked like warped wastepaper baskets, arranged in a certain way, I guessed. I don't know much about art, particularly modern art, and I don't pay much attention to it. I don't even know if this was pretty or ugly, but I enjoyed looking at it, something about the way the light was in it, the baskets made of a kind of translucent yellow-green fiberglass stuff, and sitting there with each other in their different positions like they were caught in a dance, maybe a dance at the Y, where no one dared to move till the music began. It made my mind travel, and I liked that. Maybe because it was Eva Hesse and she was from my old neighborhood, and I was proud to see it there. I mean, I had become a lawyer, big deal. But Eva Hesse, in the same amount of time, had become a famous artist. They even wrote a book about her after she died, which was a tragic death, from a brain tumor. I did see her once, just before she died, after she'd been operated on, at a party in Woodstock, New York. I was with the same client, who was becoming famous herself. "You're little Eva," I said, and I went to pat her on the head, like I used to when she was with Zoo, like I did at the dance. Some people you pat on the head; I can't explain it, like some people you pinch their cheeks. I saw her cringe, and I realized I had done a crazy thing because she had just had an operation, and I knew it, and I still tremble in my heart when I recall that gesture of mine, as if I had reached out somehow to touch her death.

"It's very sensitive," she said. "These days I get all these ideas for new work, but I can't seem to do them."

Like I said, your neighborhood will always surprise you. You never know what's going to come out of it, what stories of life and death. What greatness.

Deuce finally had his two handpainted placards set up to make it look like a bandstand—DEUCE DOUROS AND THE ACES done with glitter—and the band started its first tune, which would be repeated at least twelve times during the dance—"Blue Moon." Nobody danced. The girls stopped talking to each other and sat waiting on their side, and the boys became a little quieter, casting glances towards the girls' side, knowing something was required of them.

"Where's your sister?" I whispered to Grossman.

He pointed across the floor with his chin. She was there with a heavy girl whose mouth was ameboid with lipstick, corseted into a tight yellow skirt, and a fluffy poodle cut, on top of shapeless bluish blouse that made her look like a thick feather duster.

"Who's that she's with?" I asked.

"That's Abigail Musselman," he said.

"With your sister?"

"It's a free country. Is there a law against it?" Grossman was troubled, however. I could see the big question running down the narrow track of his mind. If she was with Abigail Musselman, did she do what Abigail Musselman did?

After the band did a sour version of "If," the terrible Perry Como song, they did "Blue Moon" again, this time with Sylvia Tweet on the vocals. Dufner was right about her. She did sound like Elmer Fudd coming out of a toothpaste tube. She actually sang it, "Bwue moon, you saw me standing awone," and she did it with a wheezing that I guess was supposed to be sexy. Her voice gave a few of the girls courage to dance with each other, and that's the way it was, girls dancing with each other, until Dufner finally got in the middle with Audrey Wolfe. She was a lean, nervous girl, who pushed her body up close against Dufner's. Dufner's eyes were closed, with this half grin on his face, but hers were wide open, and she was looking around through those dark troubled eyes, as if she half expected to be scolded for being there.

Sugarman and Florry got up and swayed in the corner, out of which Mary Ryan still stared at me. In a world without Fanwoods I might have danced with her, but all I knew was that if they did come, I wanted to be clear. I noticed Kutzer had come in, and was sitting with Press and his wife, talking grown-up talk. Grown-ups look to kids like absolutes, treading the water of life, in place, in control. I've spent the rest of my life expecting to become such a grown-up as I knew them when I was a kid. Maybe when you die it happens. Except Kutzer. He was probably never a kid. I hated him. I would like to have gone up and asked him to leave. Get off my turf, Kutzer. But forget it, it wasn't worth the trouble. Zoo was dancing now with Eva, and there were some other couples I didn't know. Stames had grabbed Abigail Musselman and she was dancing very formally with him, some distance between their bodies. Cockeyed Sydney played a squeaky solo on "Someone to Watch over Me," his eyes crossed over his clarinet. The floor was crowded enough for me now to make my move, and I started slowly across the floor to where Linda Cuebas sat next to her mother on the edge of her seat. As soon as she saw me coming she looked the other way as if she hadn't, because it wasn't cool to seem to want to dance too much.

"Play a cha-cha," Dufner shouted.

"Oh no," I said to myself.

Dufner did a few jerky glides around Audrey Wolfe. "We want to Cha-cha-cha."

My stomach began to do a lindy. It was hard enough to ask her to dance, but what if I did and they started a cha-cha? Linda certainly knew how to do that one. It was her native dance. I'd be totally faked out. I'd stand there like an idiot, like I did in the game; so instead of continuing across to Linda, I veered off to an empty spot, and stood there with my arms folded across my chest, like a supervisor too busy to dance. Mr. Press danced by with his wife.

"Those were some great shots you made in the first half, Swanny," Mr. Press said, as he passed.

"Thanks, Mr. Press. I lost it all in the second half, though."

"That kid, Coony, is too good. He scores twelve points a game for Clinton. You looked good, though. Keep it up.

That was what I needed. Mr. Press knew how to make you

feel like somebody. I walked right up to Mrs. Cuebas and asked her permission to dance with her daughter. It was easy. She said, "Of course," and I turned to Linda and asked her. Linda looked appropriately surprised, but she grinned a mile, and when the band started to ruin "Autumn Leaves" she got up and put herself in my arms and we danced. I never regretted it. This was like a revelation. It was the most tender surprise of my life, feeling suddenly that small body move with mine. Not even my first lay, or my fiftieth lay, approached the wisdom of that experience. We were so quiet with each other. I've never said so little since to someone I liked so much. She smelled like lilacs in the country, and moved as if swayed by a little wind, and was so light moving with me as I stumbled that she even made me feel graceful. My right hand held the curve in the small of her back, and the feel of it made me drunk. I'd never touched anything like that before; that indentation of the channel of her backbone, so supple, moving so easily within the slipping silks of her flesh. Its strength was startling, and its ability to stretch, to twist, to bend. She moved in ways I could never imagine moving my own body, and she leaned against my strength, making my own movement more possible. I felt like we were lost under water, swimming with one body. Swimming in a sea of inaudible music. I almost didn't hear her when she said, "You really dance good, Swanny."

We were back by her mother, and she sat down.

"I do?" I said.

"Yeah. I'm sorry I'm such a bad dancer."

"You're a really good dancer. Thank you. We'll dance again later, okay?" I looked at her mother, who was in her own reverie, a smile like a far distance on her face, her hands folded on her black lap.

The pink paper had slipped off one of the lights and spot-lighted underneath Stames and Abigail Musselman, who had dropped the formalities. She was pressed against the wall, and Stames's hands, that could palm a basketball, that squeezed a bat, that could hit the ball over the fence for us, his big hands were all over her corseted body. Juicy Lucy Grossman sat next to them snapping her bubble gum. She seemed a little con-fused, and looked around as if she didn't know if she was just supposed to act cool, or find somebody to try to stop it. When the music stopped you could hear them grunting. Mr. Press and his wife didn't pay any attention. They were all the way in the opposite corner of the room. Grossman stood next to the band and looked at them, with this expression on his face, like he was seeing his first movie, or something. His sister wouldn't meet his eye.

"Come here, Swanny."

I went over to him. "What?" I asked.

"Look, please dance with my sister."

"What for?"

"She's just sitting there. She stays there with them."

"What difference does it make?"

"They're all over each other. It's like they're humping."

"She's not doing anything. What's the problem?"

"If it was your sister you'd understand. You don't even have a sister. Dance with her, Swanny. I saw you dancing."

Dufner suddenly jumped into the middle of the band and bent over to look right into Deuce's face. "You're driving me crazy with this 'Blue Moon.' All you play is slow numbers. Can't you play some cha-cha? Can't you play a lindy? We're falling asleep with Deuce Douros and the Aces."

Deuce tried to ignore him. He repositioned his drums.

Dufner stayed right in his face. He looked like he might have
done a good job covering Coony.

"Don't you know any cha-chas?"

"I didn't bring my conga or timbales," Douros apologized.

"You're the only one here who wants a cha-cha," said Sylvia
Tweet.

"Cha-cha on this," said Dufner, giving her the finger.

"You're just a postnasal drip," said Sylvia Tweet.

"I want a cha-cha," said Audrey Wolfe.

Dufner grabbed a drumstick and started to rap on the cowbell and to sing in a voice like a ratsqueak.

"Donde? Donde stabas tu?" Dufner sang. All over the dance floor
kids were covering their ears and moaning. *"Donde. . .Stabas tu?*
Cha-cha-cha. That's one. Here's another one. 'What is the
number? I do not know the number. What is the number? Is it
number sixty-seven? That is not the number. Is it number
sixty-eight?' " Dufner stopped singing and handed the drumstick back to Douros. "I can do it. Why can't you? You're the
band."

The band squeaked through a cha-cha while Dufner and
Audrey took over the dance floor. They looked great, despite
the fact that Douros didn't have much more cha-cha rhythm
than Dufner himself on the cowbell. Dancing there they
looked like Killer Joe and Conchita the great cha-cha instruc-
tors at the Palladium. Dufner had moves while he was dancing
I never saw on the basketball court. He was cool. He held onto
his lapelless jacket and moved himself as if he was born to
dance. He could glide, spin, jump, do splits. I was impressed.
With some breaks he could have been Gene Kelly if he was
Irish and had a little more love in his heart. I could see why
Audrey Wolfe could spend time with him, though he was two

years younger, and at that age those were two big years. They both loved to dance, and made a peculiar but convincing pair. Everyone surrounded them and watched, even Stames and Abigail Musselman, who looked like they'd just been running a race. When the cha-cha ended and "Blue Moon" began again they found their spot against the wall, and went at each other again.

"Now dance with her," Grossman said, coming up behind me.

I gave in this time, and walked over to Lucy. The smell of those two kids making out was stronger than the locker room after a game. It was like being up to your neck in dirty socks. I couldn't see how Lucy could bear just sitting there in it, when she wasn't a participant.

"You want to dance, Lucy?"

She looked at me as if some stranger had come up and asked her to show him her underpants. "No thank you," she said, and looked away coldly. I think she really enjoyed turning me down. She was also a little scared by what was going on right next to her. As for me, I learned how bad making out could smell.

The dance was almost half over, and still no sign of Fanwoods. I began to think that maybe they really were going to leave us alone. I was feeling pretty good. I danced with Linda Cuebas a couple of more times. I danced with Florry once, while Sugarman was dancing with Mary Ryan. Her ponytail, her face shining without makeup. I could feel how lucky Sugarman was. Then I danced with Mary Ryan, I was so light-headed. The band was playing "Someone to Watch over Me," and I turned with Mary Ryan in my arms, and suddenly I was facing the entrance, and I saw these three guys standing in it. Everyone must have seen them at once, because there was like a change of weight in the room, and a dark silence. These three guys were big, and they were dark. Mr. Press saw them, and he stood up and started to walk towards them. The band even got quieter.

"What is it?" Mary asked, when she felt me let go of her.

"I think your brother's here," I said.

She jumped away from me as if I'd suddenly turned into the electric chair. She looked at them real carefully, then came back and took my arm to finish the dance with me. "It's not Fanwoods," she said.

"What are they?"

"I think they're Condors."

The Condors' jackets were green and white. The pink light made them look black. One of the guys was as big as two Fanwoods.

"What do you think they're doing here?"

She looked at me as if I was stupid. "I don't know. This is a dance, isn't it? That big guy I think is Tony Galupo. He likes to sing. He sings with the choir."

Tony Galupo was known as "The Crusher." If he walked down the middle of the street, trucks got out of his way.

"I wonder if they paid to get in."

Again she looked at me as if I was stupid. "The dance is almost half over," she said. "Besides, Condors don't pay to get in."

They swaggered around the room, sure that everyone knew who they were. We all tried to look as inconspicuous as possible. Only Stames and Abigail Musselman were oblivious. They stopped and watched the two make out, and looked around at everyone else with these grins on their faces. Then they tapped Stames on the shoulder.

"What?" he said stupidly, turning his head. Galupo pushed him out of the way and stepped up to look in Abigail's face, then he stepped back and turned to his guys.

"She's a dog," he said, and he pushed Stames back up against her.

Hubby came up to me, growling like a little bulldog. "We should throw 'em out, Swanny. We should all get together and kick their asses out of here."

"What for?"

"Mr. Press'll help us."

"Hubby!"

"They didn't even pay to get in."

"Hubby, the dance is half over; and Condors don't pay to get in."

"There are fifteen of us, Swanny. There's only three of them."

"I don't care if there's fifty of us. We leave them alone."

"No wonder they call the Bullets chicken."

The three Condors were standing now, looking at the band. Condors were the biggest birds in the world, and these guys looked big. You couldn't even see the band when they stood in front of it.

"They want to hear a cha-cha," Dufner walked up to the band. "Play another cha-cha."

"Can you play 'Time after Time'?" Galupo asked Douros.

"For this band time after time is too often," Dufner tried to joke, but Galupo looked at him as if he had guessed the exact moment when Dufner would die.

"How about 'Vagabond Shoes'?" Galupo asked.

Deuce had stood up and was looking through the music at Seligman's stand. "I think we've got 'Saturday Night,'" he said.

"Play it," said Galupo.

"I don't really know it," said Cockeyed Sidney. Galupo reached out and grabbed his big nose so his eyes almost disappeared into his sinuses. "Play it."

"Leave him alone, you big lug," said Sylvia Tweet.

Galupo stepped up to her and narrowed his eyes. She pulled back and punched him in the stomach. Galupo grinned. "They're all dogs at this dance." He took the microphone out of her hand, and turned to Douros. "Okay, ready. One and two and three and four." He had to go through that three times before they started, and then Seligman was lost behind the beat, missing half the notes, but Galupo sang.

"Saturday night is the loneliest night of the week. . ."

He was good. What can I say? Bernie Grossman came up to me and spoke in his most heroic voice. "I thought I was going to have to do something. I thought they were going to bother my sister."

"He sounds pretty good," I said.

"Yeah, a little like Vic Damone. I'm glad they left her alone. I don't know what I would have done."

"You might still get a chance," I said.

"You think so?"

Galupo sang with a small, mellow voice, as if within that broad body a skinny Frank Sinatra was disguised. He held the tune really well, and gave the song a nice flair. "How about 'There's No Tomorrow,'" he said, when he was done. Deuce just shrugged. "Why don't you Bullets get a band for your dance?" he asked the room. Then he sang the song without accompaniment. His Condor buddies stood on either side of him, with their arms folded across their chests like bodyguards. It was impressive. When he was done all the Bullets applauded. Even Mr. Press and his wife stood up and clapped. Galupo lifted his arm to quiet everyone down, as if he was on stage at the Paramount.

"You've been listening to Tony Galupo. I'm a male vocalist. Available for all your communions, or Bar Mitzvahs, or your next game and dance." He held the microphone out for Sylvia Tweet, but the smallest of the Condors grabbed it and shouted, "*Achtung, schweinhunds, Heil Hitler.*" Galupo took the mike away from him and put it in Sylvia's hands. The band started to play "Blue Moon" again. I don't know when the Condors left but they were gone before the dance was over. I got to dance the last few with Linda Cuebas, and Mr. Press danced with her mother, and even Bernie Grossman danced, with Mary Ryan. While I danced with Linda I watched Sugarman and Florry spin together in their corner, holding each other by the waist, and staring into each other's eyes, and turning and turning. It looked so beautiful. I don't know how they did it. I felt so light-headed and dizzy just putting my hand on Linda's tiny waist, that had I added turning in circles and looking into her eyes, I would have fallen down.

The dance was over. No big deal. Linda left with her mother. Not a Fanwood anywhere. It was over. Mr. Press turned on all the lights. So we had given our game and dance, and nothing really happened; nothing, at least, that I had anticipated, and I was the only one it seemed who anticipated anything at all like a fight, or maybe it was just me. Maybe it was something flowing only in my blood. The game and dance were over, and it had been peaceful, and what's more, at this dance, I had danced.

I waited around to help Douros pick up his drums. Mr. Press tried to rush us along because he closed the place up. "I think we sounded pretty good," said Cockeyed Sidney, before he left.

"We've got to rehearse," said Deuce. "We're not gonna get better if we don't rehearse. What do you think, Swanny?"

"I don't know," I said. "I don't know anything about music."

"Kids, let's go," said Mr. Press. "I wanna get home sometime tonight. I don't want to miss *Dagmar*.

Deuce and I walked down Fort Washington to 176th Street. His father's restaurant was on Broadway between 175th and 176th. We were going to meet Bruce Kcock there if he was through with his card game. We didn't expect him to be, but at least we would get our spumoni and biscuit tortoni out of it. About halfway down 176th Street we saw some kids in a lobby, and my first thought, of course, was Fanwoods. I started to pull Douros across the street, but one of the kids ran out at us, and it was Stames, unmistakable. Round head, round shoulders, round belly.

"Swanny, hey, come on in here. Who's that with you, Douros? You come in too. She's putting out."

"What's happening?"

"She's putting out, I said."

"Putting out what?" Deuce asked.

"She's putting out a fire. She's putting out the laundry. What do you think she's putting out? It's Abigail Musselman."

"In there?" I pointed at the dimly lit lobby.

"What's in there?" Deuce asked.

"I'll show you." He grabbed Deuce's belt and pulled him into the lobby. I followed. I knew this building. It was the Royal Arms. When you delivered flowers here on Mother's Day you didn't expect much of a tip. The walls were babyshit yellow. In the center of the lobby floor was a circle enclosed in a diamond

with the letters RA in little tiles in the middle of it. The stair-
ways went up on either side of the building. Mamoulian and
Hubby sat on the left side at the foot of the stairs.

"Where's Abigail?" I asked.

"She's under the stairs," Stames said.

"Well who's with her?"

"Hubby's supposed to be," said Mamoulian.

"I don't want to go near it. I don't want to touch it. I don't
want to see it," Hubby said.

"He's chicken," Mamoulian said.

"I looked at my mother's once. I'm not chicken."

"It's not the same thing, Hubby." Mamoulian handed us the
flashlight. "If you guys want to go first, go ahead."

"It probably smells like a pisspot," Hubby said.

Stames took the flashlight and led us like some cave explorers around under the stairway that went up to apartments A
to F. "You still there Abigail?"

"I'm here."

Stames shined the flashlight under the stairway. "Look," he
said.

"Somebody come here," she said. "I'm getting cold."

She sat in her corset on a milk crate, playing with the tips of
her hair. Her coat and skirt, folded neatly, lay at her side.
Stames probed between her legs with the light, and as if she
could feel the light prodding her she spread her heavy thighs.
The little hatch of her corset was unhooked and flapped
beneath, and somewhere in that tunnel made by the corset and
her thighs was the cause of all this conflict and excitement.

"Someone please come here," she said.

Grossman had taken his sister home, and I was glad of it. I
don't want to say anything against Abigail, because she was
doing something she needed to do at the time, and despite the

"reputation" it earned her, it was generous and good for the guys who needed it, a kind of mobile sex education class, but Lucy in her young, horny, romantic innocence, didn't need to witness this.

"So if you want to touch it, go ahead," Stames said.

"You just reach in there and touch it?" I asked.

"Yeah. She lets you."

"That's it?"

"That's what we did."

"Come on, somebody. I gotta leave in a minute. My sister gets home from work." She and her older sister, who was a waitress, lived alone together.

"Okay, I'll do it," said Douros. Stames handed him the flashlight.

"Once you find it, turn the flashlight off, so we don't attract attention," Stames instructed. "And don't make a lot of noise."

Stames and I sat down on the steps with Mamoulian. "Where's Hubby?" Stames asked.

"He went home," said Mamoulian. "And he's the one who wanted it the most."

"He's too young," said Stames. "When I was his age, I couldn't have done it either."

We heard some giggling from under the stairway and smiled at each other. "You gonna do it, Swanny?" asked Mamoulian.

I acted as if I didn't hear, as if I was trying to hear what Abigail and Deuce were saying.

"What if she clamps up?" I asked.

"On his finger?" Mamoulian said.

"Come on, Swanny. You gonna do it, or not?"

"I don't have a Trojan," I said.

Stames looked at his hand. "You put a scumbag on?"

"You should always carry one," Mamoulian said. He pulled

out his wallet. "You've got to be prepared, because something can happen any time. Like tonight. Or after a game down by the river you meet some chick. You can never tell when they're gonna get hot. I think they prefer the Ramses or the Sheiks. I never buy the Trojans." He spoke like a genuine connoisseur, and pulled the condom, molded into its foil, from his wallet, and offered it to me.

"I can't take yours," I said. It was like a real trick of courage to buy one in a drugstore. You had to step up to the counter, and try to look eighteen and blasé, although I don't think you needed to be, and hope your voice didn't crack when you said to the druggist, "I'd like to buy some condoms please."

"What kind?" the pharmacist always asked, real businesslike. If your mind didn't go blank you'd state a brand.

"They come in packs of three, or boxes of twelve." That would blow your little reserve of calm, and you'd ask for the dozen, not to seem like an amateur, and there would go a month's allowance, and you'd have a lifetime's supply.

"I've got one at home," I said.

"You should carry it, Swanny," said Mamoulian.

"Did you ever use a French tickler?" Stames asked.

Douros and Abigail came out from under the steps together.

"It has little rubber things on it."

"What has little rubber things?" Abigail asked.

"Swanny didn't get a turn," Stames said to her.

'I've gotta go home. My sister doesn't even know I went out. Besides, it's too cold under there."

"It's better in the summer," I said.

"Yeah, then you can go to the beach," she said as if it meant something really sexy. We walked out of the building, and she blew us a kiss, then stepped real sprightly down Fort Washington Avenue with her arms around both Stames's and Mamoul-

ian's waists. That's why I was never one to put her down for
doing what she did. It made her feel good, powerful, maybe, for
a little while. A little while is all even the best-looking of us can
hope for.

"I liked her," Douros said.

"What do you mean?"

"She's nice. I mean she's not the world's greatest beauty, but
at least she's hip. She digs the sounds. How many girls that you
know have heard of Fats Navarro."

"You talked about music?"

"I always talk about music, and she told me about her sister.
Her sister works in a restaurant not too far from Birdland."

When we got to his father's restaurant it was almost mid-
night. Through the window we could see Onion cleaning the
floors. Bruce was probably still deep in his poker game. Deuce
let us in with his key, and we grabbed a couple of spumonis and
tortonis each and sat down. A nice way to end the evening.

Onion mopped his way past our table. "You like basketball,
Onion?" I said.

"Pardon me." He stopped and leaned towards us, his eyes
oozing like an unhealthy dog's.

"You like to watch the boys play basketball?" I prodded him
cruelly.

He grinned weirdly, and laughed like the hunchback of Notre
Dame. "Pardon me," he said, and went on with his mopping,
stopping occasionally to look at us and scratch his crotch. You
might call Onion one of the pitiful cases of our neighborhood,
but he survived.

So nothing happened at that dance, except what happened
afterwards. Even today to tell it I have to stop because I feel this
sigh that weighs a ton growing in my throat, and a cold circuit
up my spine, as if my own ghost was moving in me. The next

morning Florry O'Neill was dead. I tell you the truth. They found her body still dressed as it had been for the dance, lying on the uppermost landing of her own building in front of the door to the roof. Whoever did it had suffocated her to death with ether, had carried her up there, had raped her there on the roof, and then carried her back inside to leave her on the landing, her shoes neatly by her side, as if the guy thought that if she happened to wake up the next morning she'd find them there in order. He had folded her hands across her chest, and when they found her the hands had lifted a little with the arms in rigor mortis so it looked like were she standing she would have been preparing to dive. She was still diving. Florry O'Neill's eyes that had startled me so much when I looked in them once—one of them green, the other half grey, half brown as I remember—were closed forever. I've seen a lot of people die since, in a lot more horrible ways; but that one was my first death, as it was, really, for most of the kids in the neighborhood, and as the poet says, after the first death there is no other.

You could taste the silence in the whole school. It was heavy, like honey, only bitter. It was this unfamiliar sound, in the usually crazy halls of Humboldt Junior High School, of solemn whispering. Everyone looked older. Everyone was experiencing her death in some way. Even Dufner, who at one point in his usual mean nerviness and bad taste grabbed Marsha Kaplan, the daughter of Mr. Kaplan the science teacher, from behind, and smushed her handkerchief into her face. Booby Oserow was there, and he started laughing, but stopped as soon as he realized that nobody else was laughing, and that everybody was actually walking away from Dufner, who suddenly began jumping in front of people and making faces like he was eight years old, clucking like a chicken. He wore out fast, and sat down on a stairway with his head in his hands, and didn't look at anybody, and he sat there all the rest of the day, didn't go to class, didn't say anything to anyone but himself.

Mr. Kaplan, Marsha's father, was the mad scientist of the school, and he was pretty numb to everything that was going on. He thought of himself as the Einstein-Houdini of the school. He liked to show off the miracles of static electricity, the wonder of bioluminescence. He made his classes into corny magic shows, where he would pick up a neon tube and it would light up in his hand. He taught all the special classes. His favorite trick he called his flea circus, where he made the iron filings dance around on a piece of paper, and had magnets arranged underneath so they ended up spelling out KAPLAN. His hair was all frizzy like Einstein's, and he walked around the halls giggling to himself, oblivious to the kids, some of them taller than he was, imitating from behind his Groucho Marx strut. Marsha, who looked a lot like him, would always try to be somewhere else when her father was in the halls.

No one thought that he would be able to start his section on the dissection of frogs the Monday after Florry died, but we sat down in the science room and there were twelve frogs hopping in a little terrarium and twelve bottles with cotton in them. As usual he wanted to turn it into a show, so he borrowed a page from Mark Twain and arranged two little alleys on the table on which we would get to race the frogs.

"This will also," he explained, "give us an illustration of Darwin's theory of the survival of the fittest." Even then that sounded hokey and unscientific to me. He lifted two of the frogs from the terrarium and placed each in a lane. One of them didn't move at all, but the other jumped immediately to the other end. He picked up the first one, that still hadn't moved, and held it under its little front legs, shining its vulnerable white belly in our eyes. "You see how ambition and activity help you live longer, but laziness . . . ." He lifted the lid off one of the killing jars and the smell of ether hit everyone at once. "No," said a chorus of students as he dropped the frog into the jar. "You cannot be squeamish if you are going to be a scientist," he said.

"Mr. Kaplan, we . . .," I tried to explain, but he interrupted me. "There will be a lot of time for questions later."

Several of the girls sneaked out of the room before he killed the next loser. By the time he was ready to kill the fittest frog just three of us were left. He looked around, took off his glasses, and blinked.

"What is this? This is an outrage. We have the frogs when we have the frogs. We don't have the frogs when you want to have the frogs. I am going to the principal."

He was okay, even apologetic, once I explained everything to him, but he still cut the last frog open to show me the little heart still beating, and he still made his little jokes: "You can't watch the kidney kid, or the pancreas pancreate," and he wouldn't let me go until he explained to me the miracle of formaldehyde.

My stomach felt like a pinball machine in the lunchroom. I couldn't look at food; in fact, nobody could eat the minestrone soup or the peanut butter sandwiches. I grabbed an apple and left the school, walked down the street towards St. Nicholas Avenue. I wanted to get away from all kids for a while. I was actually crying and didn't want to do it in front of everyone, though I could see everyone else wanted to cry as well.

It didn't even register when I saw the black jackets in the doorway as I passed, and then three of them, three Fanwoods, came out and jumped me from behind, and I turned in time to duck the baseball bat one of them swung at my head. That would have been a home run for their side. I started to run back towards school, and I don't know if one of them tripped me or if I tripped myself, but I suddenly flew head first against the curbstone of a building. I lay there half-conscious, not feeling, not listening to the thuds of their kicks against my body and the sound of the bat after it bounced off my back onto the ground. I heard one of them say, "Shit. Here comes Press," and they were gone.

I felt the hand on my shoulder, and heard Mr. Press's voice. "Can you hear me, Swanson?" I uncurled a little, slowly reassuring myself that everything could move. "Do you hear me?" Mr. Press said again.

"No I don't, Mr. Press," I said. "Do you think you could speak a little louder?"

"You jerk," he said, and gently touched my head above my right eye. It felt like there was another head in there, punching to get out.

"I don't think there's a concussion," he said. "Did you see who hit you?"

"They didn't hit me, Mr. Press. I hit the head with my wall." Even though I screwed it up, that seemed a little easier to admit.

He picked the bat up out of the gutter. "It's a Lou Gehrig model. You'd think they could hit you with this. Who were they?"

"They were Fanwoods."

"Great. Fanwoods. We'll arrest the whole Fanwoods." He grabbed my hand and helped me up. "Look I'll write you an excuse so you don't have to be here this afternoon."

"That's okay," I said. "I'll be all right." I didn't want to go home. I knew my mother would want to run me to the hospital, which I hated, and my father would give me the old lecture about getting the other guy. I sat through civics and English, my head throbbing like a pump, and my body began to ache where their kicks had landed. No one even asked me what happened. They could read the whole Florry-Fanwood-Bullet connection right off my bruises, and their seeing me changed something in the mood of the school that afternoon, as if in me they'd got a glimpse of the excitement that was coming. Noise came back into the hallways. The mourning, which after all is only a light nap for the living, especially for some kids in a school, was over, and this irresistible joy at being alive was waking everyone up. It wasn't they who were dead, after all, Florry was; and life tasted secretly sweeter with the awakening of that recognition. Though everyone did feel bad about Florry, by dismissal time there was this upbeat in the kids. They sneaked looks at my bruised face and ran home giddy, congratulating themselves secretly for still being alive.

I called home and told my mother I was visiting Mamoulian and that I was going to have dinner with him. I didn't even ask her permission, as I usually did, and that must have shocked her. But parents need to be shocked. That's the job of a kid. Then I got on the number five bus and let it take me on its long ride through the whole city to Houston Street. They still had some double-decker buses at that time, and I rode on top, right above the driver's seat, watching Riverside Drive go by, and Grant's Tomb, and Central Park, and St. Patrick's Cathedral, and the Empire State Building. It was reassuring to get into the rest of the city. I was otherwise so locked into my neighborhood. There were thousands of people on the street, cancelling each other out, reaffirming each other. And the pretty girls—dozens of pretty girls appearing one after the other framed in the window in front of my seat.

I grabbed a number four bus back, as it was getting dark. One thing I remembered about Florry O'Neill kept going through my mind. We had never ever talked that much, but I remember this one conversation we had while we were dancing.

"So what are you gonna do when you grow up," I asked her, just joking, like making fun of grown-up questions.

"I'm going to be a doctor," she said. I thought she was kidding, going along with my joke. I must have looked stupid, with my broad, patronizing grin.

"You mean you want to go to nursing school?"

"No." She looked at me with those eyes. "I'm not going to be a nurse. I'm going to be a doctor."

At first that made me feel very strange, nervous. I leaned back and looked at her. She's too pretty, went through one side of my mind, and goddamn, this is really somebody, went through the other. "Dr. Florry O'Neill," I said. "Not bad."

I jumped off the bus at 181st and Fort Washington. It was dark already. Funny how things in your own neighborhood can seem unfamiliar; like I was seeing it not only for the first time but in a different color. There was this sad yellow over everything, and everything had a tired smell, like an old lady lying in her bed. I walked down the hill to Broadway and stood on the corner. A movie would have been perfect then, but that would have got me home so late my mother would have called the police and died a thousand times. She would have made me eat. While I was standing there Dufner came out of the Coliseum with Audrey Wolfe. She was actually wearing his Bullet jacket. Dufner looked so grown-up with her on his arm, like some kind of husband at fifteen. She looked even older than seventeen, like someone who'd be going out with guys in their twenties.

"Swanny," he shouted, coming across the street.

"What'd'ja see?" I asked. It was amazing that he could go to a movie on a Monday. If I suggested it in my house it would be a big issue.

"It was Humphrey Bogart," he said. "It was *Key Largo.*"

"He doesn't like Humphrey Bogart," Audrey said.

"She always knows what I like and what I don't like," said Dufner. "And she's right. Humphrey Bogart is a creep with a big head. And he looks like he's always constipated; that's why his upper lip is tucked under. If he could take a shit, he'd relax."

"Frankie," said Audrey, giving him a little love push.

"It's true. In this movie Bogart looks constipated all through the movie. He's just holding it in. Then, near the end, this woman gives him a gun, and that's like the Ex-Lax—you know he's gonna get relief. Then at the end when he shoots Edward G. Robinson and all his hoods it's like he finally took a good crap, and he relaxes his face. Lauren Bacall opens the window to let the sun in and let the smell out."

"That's why I hate to go to the movies with him," Audrey jabbed Dufner and smiled. "He's always got some nutty idea."

"Now I don't have to see the movie," I said.

We stood there silent for a few moments, knowing what we all were thinking about.

"I was such a jerk in school today. Sometimes I'm just a jerk," Dufner said. I put a hand on Dufner's shoulder, the first time I'd ever felt anything sympathetic for him.

"It's horrible," said Audrey. "She was so pretty Saturday night. I was jealous of her."

"I danced with her," I said.

"You know what they did?" said Dufner, as we started to walk downtown.

"Who?"

"The police. They picked up Dinnerman."

"Dinnerman? Why?"

"Yeah. They locked him up."

"Dinnerman didn't do anything."

"They like to lock Dinnerman up. I guess someone saw him in the neighborhood, so the cops picked him up."

"Jesus," I said. "I hope they don't try to pin it on him."

"They just like to persecute Dinnerman because he's been in reform school, and his mother used to be a whore."

"I didn't know that."

"You got beat up, huh?"

I'd almost forgotten about it. I touched my swollen head. "A little trouble," I said.

"That's some lump," said Audrey. "Have you been to a doctor?"

"I haven't been home yet. I hate doctors."

"You should go to emergency at the Medical Center. You want us to take you?"

I ignored her and spoke to Dufner. "I guess they'll be after us a lot now."

"That's why I'm quitting the Bullets," Dufner said.

"You're always quitting the Bullets. That won't do any good."

"I'll join the Fanwoods," he said.

I thought he must have been kidding, but he didn't have a smile on his face. You never knew about Dufner, and Dufner never knew about himself.

They turned off on 176th, and I kept on down Broadway. I suddenly felt a little scared and tired. In any one of these doorways, I thought, the Fanwoods could be there. I moved out onto the street, so no one could get me from a hall. Across the street I saw the lights on inside the funeral parlor on 174th. A car was sitting in front of it, with its motor running, and someone sitting in the car. I recognized it, and stopped. It was

Kutzer's car. He slowly started moving. I crossed the street, because you know how you can have the feeling something weird is going on. Kutzer drove around the block and then kept going up Broadway. I don't know if he saw me or not. I looked through the glass doors of the funeral parlor. The light was from deep inside, from behind the black curtains. I could see some shadows moving back and forth. No way, Swanson, I said to myself, that you're going in there. Under the best conditions I don't like funeral parlors or the vultures that run them, and at that point I was just a kid and it looked spooky in there. But for some reason I stood looking in at the shadows for a long time. Then I tried the door. I just touched it and it swung open. I pulled my hand back like it had touched a live wire. I even turned my back on the place as if to walk away, took a few steps, and then turned back, and after taking a deep breath I went in. I stood and watched the shadows move for a long time and listened to the whispers. What business had I to go in there? What had drawn me? A light scent of formaldehyde drifted on the air currents. I thought I recognized the voices whispering behind the curtains. I mean, this was Inner Sanctum time for me. I breathed deeply and pushed aside the curtains. Some spotlights illuminated a body on a slab. It was Florry O'Neill's body, just her head showing from under the sheets. The lights blinded me to whomever else was in the room, then I heard a familiar, stupid voice.

"Hey, Swanny. How did you know about this?" It was Booby Oserow, standing there, his pants down around his ankles, his blue boxer shorts held up by his hard-on.

"You wanna see it?" said Ginzy the Creep, the other person in the room. He pulled the sheet off Florry's body, where it was seasoning, or whatever they called it, in its dead fluids and formaldehyde. Her father had accepted the conclusion that she had died of the ether and suffocation and had managed to keep them from cutting her open at the autopsy so her body looked good. "That costs fifty cents," said Ginzy, somewhere off behind the lights. I actually stood there looking at her like I was frozen in place, and I wish I never did because I still see her glowing like that sometimes, somewhere above my dreams.

I shook myself out of it and went over to cover her up, even her face, and I turned to Oserow. "Crazy motherfucker. Pull your pants up." I stepped and pushed him so he stumbled back into the curtains, then I pushed him through the curtains and followed. "Pull your fucking pants up and get your ass home or I'll kill you. I'll kill you, fucking kill you, and you'll deserve it."

"Swanny, I paid. . . ."

"Don't say a word. Run your fat ass home. Get the fuck out of here. Run home. Run home."

I could hear myself saying all that as if it was somebody else talking, and saying to myself, "Swanson is really pissed." I wouldn't have killed him. I might have solved his problem by castrating him at the time, and that wouldn't have been a crime, but I wouldn't have killed him. The kid was a sad case.

Oserow got out, as fast as his fat body could move. I went back through the curtain and saw Ginzy the Creep, still standing there in the lights. "Five dollars to touch it," he said. Booby had paid for it. That's what I had stopped him from telling me. I remembered Kutzer in the car. Had he been in here too? I didn't want to think about it. "Come here," I said to Ginzy.

He came over, the big, stupid grin on his face. "Gimme five dollars," he said. He was really demented, so I couldn't get angry. I couldn't touch him, the drool coming out of his mouth, his body smelling like all the chemicals they use.

"Show me the telephone," I said.

He led me into an office and turned on the light. "You have to pay to make a telephone," he said.

This was like his little store. Everything was for sale here. I put my last quarter into his sweaty palm, and he looked at it, then turned to leave me with the telephone. I grabbed his creepy shirt.

"What's your phone number?"

He looked puzzled.

"Your phone number, at home," I said.

I thought that maybe he didn't know it, but then he slowly told me, Wadsworth 7-4728, and I dialed the number. His mother answered, and I put a little rasp in my voice when I spoke.

"Mrs. Ginzburg, this is Sergeant Swanson of the 36th. Can I speak to Mr. Ginzburg, please?" She put the phone down. Ginzy was grinning, but it was wet around his shoes. He was actually pissing in his pants. His father got on the phone with this funeral director's dirge in his voice. No wonder this kid was nuts. "Mr. Ginzburg, this is officer Swanson. I've been keeping an eye on your place, and I saw some lights on in there, and the door was open so I went in. I found your son messing around with the body of the O'Neill girl. Now listen to me, Mr. Ginzburg. Her father is a good friend of mine, and I don't want any trouble, so I won't say anything about it to anyone. I want you to talk to your son now and tell him to come home. I've spoken with the precinct. I'll stay here with the body tonight."

I handed the phone to Ginzy, and this was the first time I ever saw him without his idiotic grin. Under different circumstances I might have felt sorry for him. He hung up, threw on his old overcoat, and left. I locked the door. I didn't expect it to backfire, because from the way he talked to his father I think he actually believed I was Sergeant Swanson. I put on some softer lights, and then I called Mamoulian and asked him to tell my mother, if she called, that I was spending the night with him. I knew his mother worked at night, so she wouldn't be able to talk to my mother. Then I called home and told my mother I was staying at Mamoulian's, and she gave me an argument, but I told her I was doing it, and that was that.

I went back into the room with Florry's body, and I folded the sheet down from her face, and looked at her. In the softer light, with some shadows on the face, she didn't even look dead, she looked asleep. I was glad they had closed her eyes.

"This is our secret, Florry. I promise. This is between you and me. Cross my heart." I actually crossed it, and then I started to cry, because I couldn't help it. I was chickenhearted. I was as stupid as everyone else. I said, "Swanson, what are you talking to a dead person for?" and I covered up her face and went into the front room and sat down on one of the clammy leather couches, and these sighs I'd begun with turned into dry heaves, and I was glad I hadn't eaten anything all day because I sat there trembling and heaving all through the night.

I must have fallen asleep a little bit, because I jumped up when I heard them opening the door in the morning. I waited behind the curtain where they couldn't see me, and then I said "Good Morning Mr. Ginzburg," as I sprinted out and beat it down the street. I don't think he even knew who it was, and probably didn't care, a sick businessman in a sick business. The funeral was the next day, so he finished up the corpse and went on to the next piece of business.

I expected my mother to be hysterical when I got home, but she wasn't. She was really calm. Sometimes a mother is okay. She fixed me an ice pack for my lump, and wrapped me in blankets, and didn't even threaten to take me to the hospital. Even though I was trying to act grown-up, I was still a kid, and all that attention felt good.

"When we moved in here this was a nice neighborhood," she said. "But with the element that's coming in here now, you never know. It's becoming a slum."

When my father came in for his breakfast he lifted the ice pack, looked at the lump, and sat down without saying anything. My mother called the school and said I was sick, so I watched my father eat his breakfast. He was real quiet, and I saw how delicate he was in his movements. I held this cap of ice on my head and felt like crying, like I was a baby. My heart was so full. I loved my father. It was as if this was the first time I saw how mortal and frail he was. He was beautiful. I felt almost embarrassed to be looking at him that way. Suddenly he looked me in the eyes, and grinned, and there was so much recognition in that grin, and he broke his silence.

"Just a piece of advice, my son," he said.

"Yes, my father," I said, going along with his tone, which he intended, I'm sure, to be funny. When he got formal it usually ended in a joke.

"If you are going to hit someone, try to avoid the temptation to hit him with your head."

"I hit the wall, father."

"Well," he laughed. "That should be even more futile and vainglorious."

I laughed too. I didn't even know what "vainglorious" meant, but when my father talked fancy, he was almost always being funny. We sat there laughing a lot that morning, like a father and son being two friends together, me with my lumps, him out of work, in the recognition of how ridiculous it is trying to be a man in this world.

Florry's death did not inspire a wake. It was too great a death, too premature. Nobody wanted to sit around and get drunk and crazy with this corpse, as the Irish people love to do. The funeral was at ten the next morning, and most of the school gathered outside the funeral parlor to watch the cars fill up. The Fanwoods were there in their jackets, as we, the Bullets, were in ours. The door of the funeral parlor faced the angle of the corner, and all the Bullets stood on the Broadway side of it, and the Fanwoods on the 174th, as they carried Florry out. Sugarman was one of the pallbearers, and when the Fanwoods saw him you could see this wave of anger pass through them. They looked like they could have jumped us right then if it hadn't been the funeral. Sugarman seemed really to struggle under the weight of the coffin. In a black hat and black coat, too big for him, probably his father's, he looked like a little rabbi. They loaded Florry into the back of the hearse, then everyone started to climb into the long line of limousines and automobiles idling with their lights on. The O'Neill family let Sugarman ride with them, and you could see the Fanwoods didn't like that at all. All the girls were crying and the guys were trying not to. Mr. Mortadella, Ginzburg's partner, stepped up to the hearse and slammed the door. Boom. That was that. The sky was clear blue, I noticed. "Blue skies, clear day, O why am I the only one feeling this way?" Billie Holliday's voice lay on my mind all day like a film of oil.

How could we believe it? How could I believe it, that we'd never, never, never see Florry O'Neill again. Never talk to her, never know what she would become. Dr. Florry O'Neill, wanted in surgery. Dr. O'Neill to the emergency room. *Aaaiiieee.* Florry O'Neill. Even now every day I think about you just a little, and every day in my life I am your faithful patient asking your help to cure the sickness in my soul.

The procession of cars pulled away like a stupid freight train, and everyone stood there in the street for a moment. Then the girls started away in twos and threes, until just some Fanwoods and Bullets were left facing each other across the invisible boundary. No one said anything or did anything. We could have rumbled very easily right there, but I felt this weakness, like my knees were melting, and I guess other kids felt it too. There was no juice in us, like it had all been sucked out. We just stood there and looked at each other. Nothing happened. We walked away.

After school that afternoon Grossman got jumped, Stames got thrown into the gutter almost under the wheels of a car, and Zoo barely escaped his lumps because he could run faster than any of them. They didn't get me this time, because I took an unusual route home, but it looked like this was going to go on forever. Unless something stopped it, this was going to be our lives.

It's like being an orphan to be in your neighborhood when it starts to feel that way. You feel like you've got no place to go. It's your neighborhood, and that's exactly why you are threatened. You know too much about it, and like I said, you can't understand it. And you're too well known. You're a kid, a New York Bullet, and that's where your troubles hang out. So there is no refuge, and what should feel like home feels like another planet; nothing to breathe, no safe passage. You walk down the street and check out every doorway. You swing wide around the corners, because your lumps, your fatal lumps, could be hiding there to grab you in black and silver jackets.

Zooky's was always a safe place for some reason, and you could hang out there for a little while. The Fanwoods would never go in. It was as if they were afraid they'd be automatically circumcised if they walked in there at all. About a week after Florry's funeral, I looked into Zooky's and there was Dinnerman, just sitting there, eating an egg salad sandwich as if it was every day, as if I'd just left him there a few minutes before and now I was back, except he didn't look very good. I slipped onto the stool next to him. I could see his face was swollen, and it was hard for him to open his mouth enough to fit the sandwich in.

"Give me a vanilla egg cream, Zooky," I said. "And give me a special." A special was a giant fat hot dog he cooked in a steamer. It burst in the mouth like a peach made out of spicy meat. I could afford one once a month.

"This is where I came when they let me go," he said. "Right here to Zooky's."

"They let you go?"

Dinnerman looked at me through his puffed and blackened eyes as if I must really be stupid. "Yeah," he said.

"What did they do to you?"

"They kissed me. They found my sap on me."

"And they used it on you?"

"No. They used it on each other."

My curiosity made me feel stupid, but I couldn't control it. I felt bad for Dinnerman, but didn't know how to tell him except by asking questions. "They hit you with your own blackjack?"

He chewed his sandwich slowly and painfully. I took a bite out of the special. It was like having a baby's arm in your mouth.

"You know, as soon as they let me go, I came right here. This is the only place I feel at home."

"You hear that, Zooky? You're a father."

"Yeah," said Zooky. "Father of trouble."

"So they figured out you didn't do it?" I said.

"Do what? They never thought I did anything. They just wanted to pick me up so they could work me over. They don't like me. I'm not ashamed of that."

"Is it because of your mother?"

He gave me this long, complicated, silent look that seemed to last forever, and then he went back to his sandwich.

"What about Florry? Did they tell you about that?"

"Shit," he said. He put his sandwich down and leaned closer to me. "They don't know anything about that, and they never will, or what pervert destroyed her. They'll never know. They picked up this nigger. That's why they let me go. They'll pin it on him. And they told me I had to join the Army. They gave me a week."

"A nigger?"

"I told them I'd join the Navy. Fuck 'em. I'm not going to get my ass shot out in the infantry in Korea. What is America doing over there anyway?"

"Do you think this nigger did it?" I didn't at the time usually say "nigger," and it sounded funny to me coming from my mouth, because my father was always careful to correct it. I always said "negro," but for the sake of the momentum of this conversation I used "nigger." It made me feel like I was some- one else talking.

"No. This poor nigger, he just sleeps in the neighborhood, works for Schwarzschild, that junk dealer on Amsterdam, and he sleeps in the store. Shit, he wouldn't touch anyone. But they'll probably put it on him and the bastards can make it stick. That's what happens if you're a nigger."

"Can't we do anything?"

He reached out and laid his arm on my shoulder. "Hey, kid," he said, and that was the first time he ever expressed the age difference between us. "I got nothin' against niggers. I smoke reefers with niggers at Bickfords on Saturday nights; but I'll tell ya, as far as I'm concerned, better him than me."

I couldn't control the grunt or sigh that I let out; I mean, I had to face it. We had troubles with the Fanwoods, but this was small troubles in a world full of trouble. Dinnerman grinned at me, despite the pain. "Relax," he said. "As soon as my face looks pretty again I'm gonna run in and join the Navy and get out of this stinking neighborhood. Change my life. I'll send you a card from Honolulu. As soon as my face feels good."

"Hey," Zooky came over to me. "You kids decide about your uniforms?"

"Yeah, we decided, Zooky."

"My Sophie would throw a shitfit, pardon the expression, if she knew I was going to do this with some money, but it's my own money I'm taking out. I got some investments she doesn't know about, and they're doing good. One day all you guys will come in here in your uniforms, *Zooky's Confectionery* on the back, and that will be that. That will be great. So you decided to do it?"

"We'll do it, Zooky, and we appreciate your offering. I just hope there's a few of us left after the Fanwoods."

I could see that Dinnerman knew that I meant that last

sentence for him to hear, but he didn't say a word. I could have used some advice at that point, or some help. He sat there pushing the crumbs of egg salad into his mouth.

"I'm glad," said Zooky. "I know all you kids a long time, like you were my own kids."

"It's your specials, Zooky," I said. "Your specials are really special."

"You know what they got at that precinct, Swanny?" Dinnerman said, like he'd been thinking about how to say it.

"What?"

"They got this guy, he must be six feet, and he's wider than he is tall, and he stands there in the room and he looks at you. He's not wearing a uniform, or anything. I don't know where they got him, out of a cave somewhere, or a cage, but he doesn't move. You know they don't dare let a guy like that loose on the streets, because he would flatten a whole neighborhood, just because he would enjoy it. He just stood there and looked at me. You know that look. They probably sent him to the Nazi concentration camps to learn that look, except that I think this guy was born with it. I think Nazis are born with it. His stare was worse than the way they worked me over with my own sap. I mean I didn't even feel that till later; in fact, while they were hitting me I thought 'I'm glad I never really hurt those queers when I rolled them in the hotel rooms,' and these cops were having a blast, like at the school-yard—swap—two points—swap—two points." Dinnerman laughed at this, even though it hurt his face to laugh. "But, Swanny, this guy. This guy was the big angel of death. There was nothing in his eyes, and I mean nothing. Not a tiny light. And that was more painful for me. That was a crusher on my heart, to see my own death in his eyes."

"Jesus, Dinnerman," I said. Dinnerman was like a kid who was two hundred years old.

"So I can't help you guys with the Fanwoods, Swanny."

"That's okay. It's all right."

"I want to glide from here on until I'm in the Navy. No trouble."

"I understand that."

"My face heals up and I'm gone." He looked at me. I could see that way deep in his eyes he was crying. "I know I said I'd help the Bullets."

"It's a Bullets' problem, Dinnerman. Don't worry about it."

He didn't say anything else. Alan Dinnerman, I understood, had let go of, or they had been beaten from his grip, the last few strings holding on to his childhood in Washington Heights.

Sugarman walked around like a ghost all fall. In school he'd take a seat slumped down in a far corner of every class. There was no one who had liked to play ball more than Freddie Sugarman, but the few times he played with us in the Y league you could see his heart was not in it, and soon he stopped coming altogether. I could feel for him. He was really hurting deep.

The Bullets were not the same, either. We didn't dare wear our jackets in the streets, because it made us into such easy targets. Mamoulian once just threw on his purple and gold to go to the store for his mother, and he got caught and beat up by a guy he said was big as a horse, so you know he was impressed, because he loved horses. I'd look at my jacket in the closet and think how nice it would be to wear it, to go down to the Museum of Science and Industry, for instance, but I couldn't do it.

It hurt me to see how much Sugarman was hurting. How could a kid fall in love that deep? But there was Romeo and Juliet, too. They were even younger. "Why must we be teenagers in love?" I kept singing to myself that stupid song. One day I followed Freddie Sugarman home, because I thought I knew him psychologically, and that even though he was keeping away from everybody he didn't really want to be left alone. He needed some contact. I called out his name, and he looked over his shoulder at me and kept walking. So I called out again, and he walked a little, then he stopped without looking back and waited for me to catch up.

"Freddie, look, I just wanted to tell you we're ordering our baseball uniforms."

"I know that," he said.

"It's great that Zooky is sponsoring us. His wife'll have a fit when she sees us. So you should have your measurements by next week, and then we have to find Baldeen. What happened to Baldeen? He doesn't come to any of the basketball games."

"He doesn't like basketball anymore. He decided not to coach basketball."

"You know Zooky is sponsoring us," I repeated, just to keep talking.

"I know that. Why don't you just leave me alone?" He started walking again, and I walked with him.

"So where is Baldeen?"

"I don't know. He's got a job. He works with a messenger service. He's at work."

We got to his door, and Freddie turned to go in. "Hey, Freddie," I said. "You should come out more and play basketball with us. We could have won some games if you were there."

"Yeah. Okay. Just leave me alone, okay?" He went

Okay, I thought. At least I broke the ice. You had to start somewhere. I wasn't thinking about anything but Sugarman when I got to the corner and turned to head towards my house. There were three of them—Fanwoods. I did an about-face, and sprinted up 177th towards Broadway. I figured Broadway was safer, with all the stores and people. I might have got around them and run down Ft. Wash to Barney's, but Barney might not have been open, and who knows how Barney would react to trouble. He'd probably close the shutters and hide until it was over, and later do me a favor and call the ambulance.

They chased me to Broadway, and I'd guessed right. They didn't jump me there with all those stores and people. I didn't turn back to look but could feel them still following me down Broadway. I stopped in front of Zooky's. To think of going there gave me a pang of conscience. Why should I bring my troubles down in Zooky's store? I could cross 174th and slip into the Broadway Temple, a Presbyterian church where I had spent some time as a Cub Scout; but it was only a Tuesday, and that church might be locked up. I looked back. The Fanwoods were just a few stores back, looking real casual, coming at me slowly, as if they were just window shopping. One of them was that guy I had met, Bill, Ryan's own lieutenant. I slipped into Zooky's, what the hell, and sat down on a stool. They came and leaned against a car at the curb and waited for me. I didn't see anything in their hands, no baseball bat or anything else.

"What do you want, an egg cream?" asked Molly, Zooky's wife. I didn't see Zooky in the store.

"No," I said. "I mean, yeah."

She saw me looking out the window. "Those your friends?" she asked.

"No. Well, yeah, sort of, I guess."

"You got nice friends. What kind of egg cream?"

"Vanilla, chocolate, strawberry, coffee. Whatever, Mrs. Zooky. Whatever you feel like making."

"Don't be a wise guy with me, kiddo, because I'll throw you out of the store. I'm not like Zooky. I don't put up with the juvenile delinquents."

There was an old guy sitting with a stool between us, a cup of coffee and a danish in front of him. He leaned towards me, grinning and squinting his eyes as if he wanted to tell me something. "You got money to pay for the egg cream?" he asked.

I pulled my last nickel out of my pocket and put it on the counter.

"An egg cream is seven cents," Molly said.

"Since when?" I said.

"Since yesterday. You can't give them away. Prices go up."

"I'll buy the boy an egg cream," said the old guy, pushing two cents towards the nickel.

"Don't buy the boy an egg cream. These kids don't know the value of money." She looked out the window. Bill was still gesturing for me to come outside. "Those are your friends?" she asked again.

"More or less," I said. "Where's Zooky?"

"Some friends," she said. "You're not going to have a rumble in my store, I hope."

"Where's Zooky?"

"What difference does it make, where's Zooky? Zooky's in

Florida. He went to California. What do you care? You drink your egg cream and you go home." She put down my egg cream and took my nickel, and the old guy's two cents. He slid his danish and coffee down towards me, and changed stools.

"Sonnyboy," he said. "Let me tell you something."

"Don't tell him nothing, Mr. Gottlieb. Let him finish his egg cream and go home."

The Fanwood, Bill, was at the window, still signalling me to come out. The other two guys had pulled out a pink Spalding and were playing slug on the sidewalk.

"And tell your friends to get away from my window before they break it with that ball, and you go home too."

"Listen. I'll tell you something," said the old guy. "The older you grow, the quicker you shrink. Believe you me." His breath smelled like something had died in his mouth. "And the trouble with this neighborhood is there's too many Goimans here. Too many big shots. It's like the Nazis here."

"Shame on you, Mr. Gottlieb. You're German yourself with a name like Gottlieb. A Jewish man."

"I'm not a Goiman."

"Gottlieb isn't German?"

"They gave me that name at immigration. I came here from Lithuania, and they didn't understand my name when I said it, so they put down Gottlieb." He said his real name, and I didn't understand it either.

The pink ball hit the window, and Zooky's wife almost jumped over the counter and ran to the door. "Get away from my window, you juvenile delinquents. Get away before I call the police. You're going to break it, and then who's going to pay for it? Your father's going to pay for it, that's who."

It felt great to see the Fanwoods move down the street at the orders of little Mrs. Zooky.

"You know what I was when I came to this country? I was nothing. I came here with the shirt on my back. So foist I became a paintner. I was a paintner. You know what is a paintner, sonny boy?"

"Mr. Gottlieb, the boy didn't come here to hear your life story. He wants to finish his egg cream, and he wants to go outside with his friends."

"I've got two cents invested in his egg cream, and I'll give him my two cents worth."

"Thank you, Mr. Gottlieb," I said. As far as I was concerned he could talk forever. "You see they're really not my friends, Mrs. Zooky."

"They act like your friends. They look like your friends."

"A paintner paints the apartments. It's the foist job you loin. You loin in half an hour to become a paintner. Now I'm a carpenter; I mean, I retired, but I made a lot of money as a carpenter.So a paintner you learn to use a brush, you have a ladder, a bunch of rags..."

"O look who comes in now."

It didn't register with me. I sat focused on Mr. Gottlieb, hoping the Fanwoods would go away. If it happens this time, I thought, I'm going to fight back, thinking it through my father's mind. At least one of them is going to go away damaged. But my other side reminded me there were three of them, and I would be the one who got damaged, especially if I hurt someone and got them angry.

"See my brother, he was a peddler. That's how I found out about this neighborhood. He used to come here. You hoid him, probably. He bought old clothes. 'High cash clothes,' he used to

sing it out when he walked up the street. He had a voice like a
crow. See I always thought it was better to have a trade. But
my brother, he put two kids through college by buying and
selling those rags. One is a lawyer, the other's a dentist.
Couldn't do that in the old country. A woman is a lot of
trouble, you know. That's why I never got married, you know.
I made a lot of money." I looked in his old wrinkled face. I think
it was the first time anyone had listened to him for a long time.

"See I didn't live in this neighborhood foist. I came here, and
I didn't know about all these big shots, these Goimans. They
don't even speak Yiddish. I think I'm with the Nazis. I get
scared."

"So what do you want, you?" Molly talked to Fanwood Bill
standing behind me.

"Come on, Swanson," he said. I turned around. "Let's get
out of here. We're not going to hurt you this time. Ryan wants
to talk to you."

"To me?"

"You going to order something, or you just going to stand
there like a bump on a log?"

He pulled on my arm. "Let's go."

"So that's what a paintner is, Mr. Gottlieb?"

"What?" said Mr. Gottlieb, leaning back, already somewhere
else in his mind. "One egg cream isn't enough for you?"

Bill pulled me back off the stool.

"No rough stuff in here, you see." Molly waved the telephone at us. "I'll call the police."

"Come on, Swanny."

"Why me? Why does Ryan want to talk to me?"

"Come on."

"Goodbye Mrs. Zooky, Mr. Gottlieb. Just tell Zooky I was

here." I didn't like the feeling I felt, like helpless, like against my will.

"Good riddance," said Mrs. Zooky, as Bill the Fanwood pulled me out the door by my sleeve. It was just four o'clock. You could feel the days shortening up, a little chill in the air. The Chinese restaurant next to Loewes already had its neon on, and so did Hilfer, the Kosher butcher, and Ray Drugs. I felt like it was already night within myself, like I had been stripped naked, a slave to what was happening. One of the guys ran ahead, so there were just two of them, one on each side. I let the thought pass that I could probably handle two of them and get away. I would talk to Ryan, if that's what was going to happen. Okay. Talk to him.

I thought they were taking me back to the clubhouse, but we didn't get that far. Ryan was waiting for me on a stoop near the corner of St. Nich and 175th. Bill led me up to him. "This is the guy, right?"

Ryan looked at me, smiling. "How you doing, Swanson? Sit down." He signaled the other two guys to leave, and I sat down next to him. We were alone, as far as I could see.

"How many guys you got, Swanson?"

"What do you mean?"

"Count 'em. Close your eyes and count the Bullets. How many?"

I did a quick tally in my head, decided not to count Oserow or Douros. "About sixteen," I said.

"That's all you got," he said. "We got sixteen just on this block. Okay. This Saturday at two o'clock we'll meet you, sixteen of us, on Haven Avenue, at the steps to the river."

"What for?" It sounded like he was planning a picnic.

"No knives. No guns. I told you that. You know what for."

"Ryan, we don't have to do this."

"We have to do this. If you don't do it we'll destroy you one at a time. We'll find you one at a time, punk by punk, and you'll keep the hospital busy. You haven't felt anything yet."

"Hey, Ryan, no one feels worse than we do about Florry. It wasn't our fault. You can't blame us. It won't help anything to fight about it."

"I didn't bring you here to argue with you, Swanson. I'm telling you what'll happen."

"But why should anyone get hurt about it any more; I mean, Freddie Sugarman loved Florry. He couldn't even help that, he loved her so much. He looks like he died himself, now. None of us ever wanted anything like this."

"It was your dance. If she hadn't of been there, if she wasn't with a Bullet, it wouldn't have happened."

I caught my breath. It was hard to argue with that logic.

"Saturday. Two o'clock. We'll go down by the lighthouse under the bridge." He squeezed my arm in an almost friendly way. "A little rumble will do your Jewboy friends some good."

"I'm a Jewboy, Ryan," I said.

"That's right."

He offered me his hand to shake and I shook it. What could I do? He walked away accumulating Fanwoods from all the doorways between St. Nich and Amsterdam like a black cape trailing him. I watched them with this funny feeling in my heart. What did I have against any of them? Why did they want to hurt us? Why would we want to touch one of them? Saturday, I thought. Pray for an earthquake, a tidal wave. Pray for the Chinese to invade.

I forged a note about a doctor's appointment the next day so I could take off from school in the afternoon. It was sunny and almost warm, with a light breeze that came, it seemed, from an untroubled place to touch your soul. I walked to the George Washington Bridge. That bridge always meant a lot to me, and though I pretty much stay in one place, it always figures in my sense of where I'm going. I headed out across it on the pedestrian ramp. There weren't many cars on it at midday, and they were going slowly in my direction into Jersey because repair trucks had closed down a couple of lanes. I kept my face turned to the river in case a truant officer happened to be crossing the bridge. My favorite spot was the exact center—one foot in New York, the other in New Jersey. Out there you could feel the whole span swaying over the Hudson, and from the ramp I was on you could look upstate towards Albany. A tug pulled a line of barges down the river under the bridge, full of some reddish crap. Under the Palisades on the Jersey side the rich people had their yachts tied up. A few sailboats cruised on the river like white commas. Everything was so peaceful. All over the Palisades the trees were doing their autumn tricks. What colors. Brighter than a comic book. What unbelievable colors. "Forget about it. Forget it," I said, half in New York, half in New Jersey. Right then it would have been easier to jump off the bridge than almost anything, and I would have been happy falling into the balmy moments of blue sky and gentle wind and painted cliffs and sailboats on the river. Nice idea. End it right there. I headed into New Jersey like it was a different state of mind. I would keep going West. One day I would just keep going West, get out of Washington Heights and those battles there, out of New York City, which it seemed to me was poison for the heart and mind, and I'd go to Pennsylvania, to Chicago, to California.

The streets were sure empty in Fort Lee, New Jersey. No one was alive there. Some people worked in a few stores but were almost invisible. When I read in the *New York Post* a few months later about juvenile delinquency in Fort Lee, about sex and teenage girls in Paramus, I couldn't believe it. I mean, I'd been there once.

I took a street to the park that led back towards the river, and leaned on the wall looking out from the Palisades across the Hudson to Washington Heights. It was so small back over there. I tried to pick out the street my house was on, but all I could do was guess. I could make out Castle Village, north of the bridge, because it was a lot of big buildings, and I could see what was probably Fort Tryon Park up there, with the cloisters. And down the river there was the good old Empire State Building. Who could miss it? And the Chrysler Building, backing it up. You could see them from California, big spindles going up on which were spiked all the unpaid bills of the world. But Washington Heights? Who would ever notice it from the Jersey side? What could go on in there among those nondescript brick buildings? I could make out the lighthouse all the way across the water next to the bridge tower. Was that where our "rumble" was going to be? From Fort Lee, California, it wouldn't look like anything. Some little mice having a picnic. Some rabbits folk dancing in the open air. Okay Empire State Building. McGraw-Hill Building. Okay Island of Manhattan. Okay. So I love you anyway, place that I live in, slum of the heart, open kidney of the world, seven million bowels moving once or twice a day. What the hell. I felt so peaceful. A smile crawled across my face by itself. I looked up. Here I was under this giant tree, a maple, I think. I hadn't noticed it before. All around my feet were its flaming red leaves, and all along its branches red and orange leaves letting go in a light downward dance of pure color. "Hey tree. Hey big tree," I said. The color was like my blood turned inside out of my body and given back to the world. I slipped down and leaned against the trunk and looked through a crack in the wall at what might have been Washington Heights, and I covered myself with the blood-red leaves of my blood, and my head slipped forward on my chest, and there I fell asleep.

When I woke up I was still in the same place, and the sun was catching a few clouds in the west. It was getting late. I headed back across the bridge on the downtown side. It must have been after four. School was over by now, anyway. The air was a lot colder. All the way down the river a big freighter was finding its way north. I walked slowly, started to see my neighborhood take shape—the little park, the little houses. I reached midriver, the sign dividing New York and New Jersey, and I saw some guys on the ramp coming at me from the city. All I could see was their black jackets. I could even make out over there now the little terrace of Jayhood Wright Park, and my street, 173rd, on the south flank of the park; but how would I get there safe? I couldn't fly there. I looked over the rail of the bridge to see if there was somewhere I could climb. Too risky. I looked at the big cable, with its thinner cables going up like handrails on each side. I could climb that and battle them off at the top of the tower, like King Kong. I looked again at the Fanwoods coming, and thought, holy shit, this is for real. You could die on the George Washington Bridge, falling off the bridge. I could either go forwards or backwards. If forwards, the tactic would be to run at them all of a sudden, full speed, and break through, and head for the city. If backwards, I would get back to the Jersey tower, where the walk turned some corners and there was a platform, and I'd have a little more room to operate inside the structure, a little less chance of getting thrown over the rail. I thought too of getting in the middle lane of traffic, that was speeding like hell, and running towards New York. Something would happen then, if a car didn't hit me right there. At least maybe a cop would get interested.

I turned and sprinted for the Jersey tower. I could feel the black jackets coming after me. This time I wasn't going to give it up without a fight. I was going to get at least one of them, at least an eye, or an ear. They had hurt me enough already. I turned the corner, and pulled myself back behind a girder in the superstructure of the tower. I fit snugly into the silver channel of the girder and listened for them. The lights were coming on on the bridge, filling the air with metal. I could hear their footsteps. They were talking very softly. I closed my eyes and clenched my fists. "Fuckin' Fanwoods. I hate the fuckin' Fanwoods." I felt them close, right there. I could smell them. I jumped out to throw myself against any one of them who was closest. Destroy this fucker, I was thinking. I bounced off this big guy. A woman shouted, "O Christ. O Johnny, shit." The guy grabbed me and lifted me off the ground then threw me down. He would have shot me if he had a gun. The woman grabbed him around the neck. When he saw I was a kid alone he relaxed.

"You'll get yourself killed some day pulling shit like that."

I looked around. I couldn't believe it. I had turned this couple into all the Fanwoods; this couple taking a walk to Jersey. They weren't even wearing black jackets, not even dark clothes. My eyes must have gone crazy. Two people, and I saw Fanwoods. Lots of them.

"Did you see any other kids on the bridge?" I asked.

"You better get home, kid. Your mother's looking for you."

They walked away, and I headed back over the way I'd come. There was a sunset at my back, one of those purple ones made prettier by all the stuff in the air. I felt sick of myself, stupid; that dull sense of shame that comes when you look into the heart of your life and see it controlled by one stupid obsession. This has got to stop, I thought. One way or another.

Stames said he'd show up on Saturday, with two baseball bats, because he had his scores to settle, and Hubby, of course, practically snarled with pleasure at the idea. He would have done it alone. His brother wasn't so enthusiastic. He was studying a lot, drifting away from the Bullets, because he didn't have the natural smarts, and he wanted to go to Bronx Science and to continue from there to struggle all the way through medical school so he could be a doctor and make money ruining the health of a lot of people. It was a good thing. The way his little brother was going they would probably need a doctor in the family. Mamoulian said he had to go to the dentist at the time. What dentist gives appointments at two o'clock on a Saturday? Zoo said he didn't see any reason to fight anybody, and he wouldn't come. He didn't believe in fighting. Schletzbaum said it was Saturday, and he didn't fight on the Sabbath. He never minded pitching on a Saturday before. I didn't mention it to Oserow. Other Bullets had other excuses. Dufner said seriously (he had become very serious since he started seeing Audrey Wolfe) that he was going somewhere dancing with Audrey that Saturday night, and he didn't think they'd let him in if he looked like he'd been in a fight.

"Come on, Dufner," I said. "Just once we've got to fight

them. We've got to do it. Just to get it over with."

"You've got to fight them, Swanny. Not me. I'm quitting the Bullets. I'm a lover, not a fighter."

I didn't say anything to Sugarman. He was like the bulls-eye on a target. The rest of us were sure to take most of the punishment. So I counted three of us, and then maybe this other kid, Grossman, who had started playing ball with us, though he never came to a dance, or to hang out. His father was a longshoreman, and his mother worked too, and they were raising him to be an accountant or a college professor. He said he'd come, but I didn't believe it.

I couldn't blame anybody for not wanting to show up, for saying it was stupid. Everyone knew that all we had to do was be careful and wait it out a little longer. We'd all be sophomores in high school, probably not even in the neighborhood. It would pass. Other battles would take its place on the block. Maybe it was important just to me. Maybe that had something to do with my family, the mixture in my blood. It had become my fight more than anyone's; more than Sugarman's. More important to me than even the Fanwoods, for whom a fight with us must have been like some candy on the table.

So Wednesday went, not slow enough for me, and Thursday disappeared, and it was Friday. I could tell my mother knew something was going on the way she worked at getting me to eat. I couldn't. Food dropped like chains in my stomach. I lay awake all night with my radio next to my ear listening to Symphony Sid. He played Dinah Washington—"Love for Sale"—about six times. I hated it. But he played a lot of Stan Kenton too; Jolly Rogers, with Shorty Rogers on trumpet. I could have marched into any war to Stan Kenton's music. And he played some George Shearing—"Pick Yourself Up"; and

Stan Getz—"My Funny Valentine"; and Charlie Parker with Strings—"Just Friends." I remember them all. I didn't sleep; at least, not much. In the morning I tried to eat some Cheerios with bananas, but it wouldn't go down. I looked at my dad at the table. He had just got a job a few days before as a night watchman so he was ready to go to sleep. I would have given a lot to be able to talk to him about what was going to happen, but how? In what language does a son talk to his father about his own little wars? His struggle was to keep us going at all. My battle with the Fanwoods was a little thing, a tiny thing. I dozed off in my room around noon, and jumped up at twenty to two, only because my mother had started the vacuum cleaner. I threw on my Bullet jacket, and I was gone.

Just Hubby was waiting in front of Barney's when I got there.

"Look," he said and started unwrapping a handkerchief from around a pair of brass knuckles. "Look at these." They made me feel sick to my stomach.

"What are you going to do with those?" I asked him.

"Didn't you bring anything? A baseball bat or nothing?"

It suddenly hit me, what was going to happen; what "it" was. Hubby understood it better than I did. He had it in his bones; that to such a rumble you bring a baseball bat and swing it at somebody's head. Suddenly, right there in front of Barney's, notwithstanding that somebody had swung a Lou Gehrig model Louisville Slugger at me once, I realized that was what was going to be happening. I looked into Hubby's grin and felt weak in the knees. I saw Stames coming down 174th carrying two baseball bats, then I heard a familiar voice behind me, "Swanny. Swanny." It was Zoo.

"I didn't think you were coming," I said.

"I thought about it," he said.

"If I thought about it I probably wouldn't be here," I said.

"Yeah. But I thought I ran away on you last time, so this time I'd make up for it."

"You kids aren't still playing baseball?" asked Barney, sticking his head out the window. "It's too cold now."

"That's right, Barney."

"Next spring you'll play again."

"What time is it?" I asked.

"A little after two," Zoo showed me his watch.

"I guess it's just four of us," I said. "You better let Barney hold on to your watch."

Zoo took his watch off and handed it to Barney. "What's this for?" Barney said.

"I'll come back for it," said Zoo. "Just hold it for me, okay?"

"I close at three-thirty."

"I'll get it tomorrow."

"Sunday I close at noon. I sell the *Times*, then I close."

"It's okay if you keep it till Monday, Barney."

"I hope this isn't a hot watch. I don't want any trouble. I hope you kids aren't stealing watches."

"Barney, it's my birthday watch. It keeps good time. I don't want to break it."

"I won't break it," Barney grinned. "But I might sell it on ya."

Four of us started to walk slowly down towards 176th Street, where we turned and headed for Haven Avenue. It was a cloudy day. The air smelled faintly of New Jersey. We could see all the way from Fort Washington to the wall along the cliff of the Palisades. It didn't look like any Fanwoods there.

"They better show up," Hubby said.

"Hubby, you're crazy," said Stames. "We're all crazy to go

down there. Where's big brother Jackobitz, anyway?"

"He had to study, I think. I don't know."

"Tell you the truth, Hubby," said Stames. "I hope all the Fanwoods have to study too. I don't care if they don't show up."

"I've never been in a rumble before," said Hubby, as if we were going to the amusement park.

"That kid should be a Fanwood, or a Condor," I said to Zoo.

"I'm a New York Bullet," said Hubby, tapping the B on his jacket. "And so are you. You should be proud of it."

Zoo and I shook our heads. I think it struck us both at the same time how crazy this was, to be New York Bullets, and then to have to go get yourself damaged because you took that name and put on some jackets. It was like having to go to Korea or something.

"Someone's there," said Hubby, as we turned the corner.

We saw a couple of Fanwoods leaning against a wall near the steps. Jack Ryan appeared from behind the wall as we got closer. There were four of us, three of them.

"You should hide your shit when you come." Ryan pointed at Stames' baseball bats.

"Where's the rest of you?" I asked.

"We're here. Don't worry. Where are your guys?"

"We're here too," I said.

"Okay," he said. "Good. We'll see you in a minute, under the bridge by the lighthouse, and you'd better fuckin' be there." The three Fanwoods took off running down the steps, followed by others coming like rats out of every corner. We watched them run down the ramps and across the highway.

"Looks like shit going down a sewer," Hubby said.

"I guess we'd better follow it," said Stames.

We looked at each other. "Well, what the fuck," said Zoo, and we started towards the river too. Four of us. We were crazy to do it, like the charge of the light brigade into the valley of death.

The valley of death was under the bridge, and it was full of black jackets. They were everywhere. Zoo laughed when he saw it. "I don't believe this." There must have been forty-five of them there, standing on the abutment of the bridge, on the big rock that the lighthouse sat on, at the edge of the woods going up the hill, on the rocks by the river, everywhere. We were like four explorers walking into the middle of some cannibals. I looked across the river. I couldn't see the tree I'd slept by, couldn't make out Fort Lee, New Jersey.

Slowly they started to close in. It was like the movies, *The Wild Ones*, those black jackets tightening up on us. They all had their bats, their brass knuckles, you could hear the chains rattling, everything they needed to annihilate us beautifully.

"Jesus, Swanny. What are we doing here?" Zoo said. I looked at him. His dark face seemed like it was off in another world. I felt as if I wasn't there either by the river under the bridge.

"Don't worry," said Stames. "They can only kill us once."

"What do you mean?" Hubby asked. He was finally getting a little scared. I put a hand on his shoulder. I felt peculiar myself, but I can't say I was scared. I knew that something was going to change after this, whatever happened. Change was what I wanted, whatever change. "Fuck," I said, pulling Hubby close to me. "If it's gonna happen, it's gonna happen."

"What?" said Hubby. "What do you mean?" I could feel the tension in his body as he tried to get his courage.

Jack Ryan came out of the circle and walked up to us.

"Where's your sixteen Bullets?"

"How about your sixteen Fanwoods?" I said, swinging my arm around the heavy circle of his buddies.

"Well you know these guys." He was smiling. I'd seen that smile before. It wasn't friendly. "You talk rumble on Amsterdam Avenue and you just can't keep them away." He kept smiling at me like a Jap in World War II movie, and then suddenly he threw a shot that went right for my face, but I turned and it glanced off my cheek. The others took that as a signal to jump us, but Ryan raised his arms and stopped them.

"You felt one of them before," he said to me. "Didn't you? I don't use dusters. I don't need a baseball bat. I don't need chains."

There was this sound next to me, like this squeaking trying to be a roar, and suddenly Hubby flew like a shot at one of the biggest of them. "Four of us. Four of us," he shouted. "Four Bullets and we'll fight every one of you guys. We'll kill you." He climbed on Kevin and started to pound him. Kevin threw him to the ground like he was taking off a shirt. Hubby jumped back up and went at him again.

"Hubby," I said. "Quit it." But there was no stopping him. He just threw himself into the face of it. That's how he was. This time Kevin had a little more trouble shaking him off. Then Hubby started circling this giant Fanwood. "Hubby. C'mon," I said. "Stop." But there was no calling him off. It would be like calling David off Goliath. He circled, and made this weird noise. He was focused on it like a cat, and everybody felt it. They closed in to watch.

"If you make one move to help him," said Jack Ryan, "we'll bury you right here." I kept feeling like the movies, like I'd heard all these lines before.

Hubby circled big Kevin, who was grinning, and looking back at his companions like he thought it was a joke. "Hey don't step on him, Kevin," someone shouted.

A mistake Kevin made was to keep looking at his friends, because every time he took his eye off Hubby, Hubby bounced in and pounded at Kevin's big gut, and Kevin would make a grab at Hubby, but Hubby was gone.

"Hey, Kevin, maybe you should have brought the Flit."

"Yeah, or a flyswatter."

Kevin lunged and missed, and lunged again. Hubby easily got out of the way, and threw a couple of shots into the kidneys as the big guy passed. Stames, Zoo, and I stood right next to each other, touching for security. The Fanwoods around us leaned on us occasionally because they wanted us to do something they could figure was a "move," to break their little rules, so they could jump us.

Hubby flashed in and laid a few quick shots into Kevin's gut and got away before Kevin could make a grab at him.

"Don't let him bite ya, Kevin."

Hubby was strong, even though he was small. You could see Kevin's grin getting dimmer as a look of stupid consternation crawled across his face. And you could see Hubby getting more confidence, maybe too much, as it seemed the big guy would never get at him.

"Get on your knees, Kevin, and look him in the eye."

He turned to look at the guy who said that. Kevin looked big and stupid like the big guy in *Of Mice and Men*, Lon Chaney, Jr., except unlike that guy, Kevin liked to hurt someone. "Yeah, on your knees," the other guy said.

Kevin did it, got on his knees. Hubby laughed and went right at him, and that was a mistake because he was too cocky and he tripped, and Kevin grabbed his sweater and pulled him in.

"Dance with the little fairy, Kevin."

Hubby was helpless against Kevin's chest. He squirmed a little but Kevin had him clamped. Then Kevin lunged forward, and landed on top of Hubby.

"Jesus, let's stop this," Stames said, looking around at the Fanwoods who were enjoying it.

"Shut up, Stames. You'll make it worse," I said. I had to admit that while Hubby was getting the best of him we were enjoying it a lot. "Come on, Hubby," I said.

Kevin bounced a few times on him, like the Carolina Crusher putting a steamroller on Gorgeous George. Hubby was still squirming, not hurt too much yet. Kevin got to his knees again, and leaning on Hubby with his left hand, he lifted his right to drop a punch on him. Hubby rolled enough just as the punch fell so Kevin missed, and his big fist hit a rock, and it shocked him, and Hubby squirmed loose a little, but Kevin grabbed him again, and this time stood up with him, and lifted Hubby above his head, squirming and kicking. He walked around the circle of Fanwoods.

"Throw him to me, Kevin. Toss it over here."

"Shit," said Zoo. "He could kill him."

"Make him put the kid down," I said to Ryan. "Before he kills him."

"That's right," said Ryan. "Put the kid down, Kevin."

Kevin stopped and looked at Ryan. Everyone was silent. Then he threw Hubby with all his strength to the ground. Luckily he landed on some soft grass, and rolled, and was on his feet in a second. Kevin was winded from the effort, standing there, puffing. Hubby shook himself out a little bit, took one look at Kevin getting his wind, and launched himself into the air, flew right at Kevin's face, cracking Kevin's jaw with the top of his forehead. I mean he nailed Kevin with his head. You could hear the big guy's jaw crunch out of joint. Kevin crumbled. Little dreambirds flew out of his eyes, and he fell to his knees this time, and as if all his weight was shifting to one side he slowly toppled. Hubby snarled like a little bulldog, and fell on him, pounding away. Kevin was out. His jaw was broken. Hubby would have gone for the jugular. I had to move in and pull him off, and it wasn't easy to do. The Fanwoods were stunned. They looked at their giant on the ground and were totally silent. Something had changed.

"This is bullshit," Ryan said to me, finally. "Where are the rest of your guys?"

"Look," I said. "There are no more of us. This is the Bullets right here." I said this loud enough for all of them to hear. "What happened to Florry, none of us wanted it to happen. Florry wouldn't want us to fight."

Ryan turned his back on me. Kevin finally started to get up. Hubby leaned against Stames, trembling, looking like the little tiny kid he actually was. "Let's just call it off," I said. Something hit my arm, a piece of dogshit someone had thrown at me.

"Hey, what does a kike eat for dinner," someone shouted.

"Dogshit. Kosher dogshit," several others responded in unison.

Ryan was consulting with some of his lieutenants. One of the Fanwoods, about my size, stepped up and started pushing on me. "So you're gonna tell your mother on us. You don't want to rumble. You don't want to fight."

Ryan stepped between us. "We didn't come here to play potsy with you, Swanson. We'll give your guys five more minutes to get here. Five minutes for the rest of the Bullets, and then we'll finish it with as many of you as you got here." Ryan gave a signal, and everybody drew back from us, about twenty feet. We watched them. It was as if for a moment we didn't exist for them. "I can't time it," said Zoo. "Barney has my watch." They horsed around with each other. Some of them gathered around Kevin, who was suffering, holding his jaw, and made fun of his fight.

Those were long minutes for us. It was like we were ready to be put in the pot and boiled by some cannibals. Hubby was trembling, holding back his tears.

"You feel okay, Hubby?" I asked.

"I feel okay," he said. "It's getting cold."

"Hubby you did a great fight. I couldn't believe it," Stames said.

"What'll we do?" Zoo asked.

"You got two minutes," Ryan shouted.

"He was too big," Hubby said. "I nearly got crushed."

"We'll just . . . shit. . . ." I felt really weird, not scared, just weird. "I don't know, Zoo. This is my fault. It was all my idea to do this. I don't know what I felt like. I felt like a fuckin' hero or something."

"It's not just you, Swanny . . ."

"One more minute."

One minute till what? What were they going to do? Were all of them going to hit us? Even if we were fighters, what could we do against a whole mob of them? And what could they get out of it, beating up four guys? Was that a "rumble?" Could they be proud of that? They looked bored, in fact. They paid little attention to us, although we were paying all our attention to them.

The minute was up, and the Fanwoods didn't move. Jack Ryan wasn't even looking at us. He watched someone else who had entered from behind. Stames turned. "It's Sugarman," he said.

Sugarman walked right up to Ryan as if we weren't there. He was wearing his Bullets jacket gold side out. He had nothing in his hands.

"Freddy," I said, but he didn't hear me, or didn't pay any attention. He walked right up to Jack Ryan, and the two of them stood there looking at each other.

"Sugarman," Stames shouted, but the name disappeared like some smoke into the tower of the bridge. He and Ryan looked at each other. Everything was suddenly like a dream, moving very slowly. They stared at each other forever.

"Kill me," Sugarman said, and everybody heard it.

As if a weight had suddenly fallen through my body I sank to my knees, and then folded my legs under me and sat there. Stames and Zoo and Hubby all looked at me and sat down too.

"Kill me," Sugarman said again in this voice that could cut the setting sun in two. "I don't give a shit. I'm dead already. Just kill me. Kill *ME*." Jack Ryan looked away, up at the sky.

This was too much. I looked across the river again towards Fort Lee and imagined I saw there that very tree with scarlet leaves where I had been asleep.

"Kill him," said one of the Fanwoods. "Kill the fuck."

"I don't even want to fuckin' live. Kill me. Here." Sugarman fell to his knees and lowered his head. "Do it."

Ryan shook his head. He looked at the four of us sitting down and shook his head some more. "Fuck this," he said. "Forget it." He turned his back on the whole scene and started to leave. The Fanwoods looked confused at first but then started to follow him. He stopped once, and turned to me, and pointed his finger. "You, Swanson. You motherfucker."

I don't know why he did that, as if he was blaming something on me. But it was almost friendly too.

They all followed him, not even looking back at us again. Maybe it wasn't worth it to them, finally. Or maybe it was Hubby. Maybe the rumble had been his, and he had won it for us. It seems to me now that Ryan had actually wanted to get out of it. Maybe it was too easy, too cheap a fight for him, proving nothing for him. Maybe there was some love and understanding after all in his New York Irish heart. Maybe old Einstein looking down at him every day in the clubhouse had an influence after all, a peaceful influence.

I think he actually wanted something to happen to release the Fanwoods from having to lower the weight of forty plus of them on only four of us. The gods of rumble had been gratified with Hubby against Kevin, and Sugarman had sprung the lock on the gate so they could leave.

"I'm dead anyway," said Sugarman, when we went over to get him.

"Bullshit," said Stames, lifting him onto his feet.

"I don't fucking care," said Sugarman.

"That's right. You don't fucking care," said Stames.

"You guys are assholes, that's all. You're all assholes."

We walked down to 168th Street to take the long way back to Fort Washington Avenue, just in case the Fanwoods changed their minds and were waiting for us somewhere in the bushes along the paths up to 176th Street.

*　*　*

Dinnerman looked cleaner than he had ever looked in his life, his head shaved down to his shiny scalp that had a big brown birthmark on it. The waiting list for the Navy was too long to satisfy the precinct, so he joined the Army and volunteered for the Airborne. He was a brute in that uniform, with the pants tucked inside his combat boots, the airborne patch and a stripe grinning off his sleeve. I almost didn't recognize him on the street. He looked healthy. He looked invulnerable. He looked ready to go to war.

You know it's a war when it drags on through the winter, even if someone is trying to tell you it's a police action. I mean, who would fight through the winter unless he had to? The Chinese had invaded, and driven the Americans back of the 38th parallel. Police action. Anyone close to being drafted, or close to someone who was dying out there, saw through that one. Times like that make you ashamed to be a human being. What a miserable species. Chimpanzees don't make war. The hippopotamus is peaceful. Only humans kill each other like that, sitting out in the snow, waiting to shoot your gun in the face of someone you don't even know.

"They say the Chinese come at you in human waves," I said to Dinnerman on the corner. He stood up so tall I had to speak uphill to him. "They say they don't value human life."

"I don't believe that," said Dinnerman. "Nobody wants to die."

"What about the kamikazes?" I said.

"It's cold as a bitch over there now," said Dinnerman. "That's what I heard from some guys. You freeze your nuts off sitting round in foxholes."

"I didn't think they had foxholes in Korea. Do they have foxholes?" Another stupid question from Swanson that he didn't answer. I looked at him hard. Shaved and cleaned up he looked a little more like a kid, even though he was impressive in the uniform. It was hard for me to believe he was going somewhere where he could be killed, that this could be my last look at him.

"Let's go to Zooky's," I said. "I got some good tips last weekend with the flowers. I'll buy you an egg salad."

"You know I don't even mind the idea of being shot at," he said. "I mean I'll dodge the bullets if I can. But I hate the idea of being cold. Isn't that weird?"

"Who is this I see?" asked Zooky when we walked in. He leaned forward and squinted at Dinnerman. "I can't believe it. You look like your mother loves you. You look like a different person."

Dinnerman smiled, not only at the remark about his mother, but because he didn't mind looking good. It was something new for him, getting compliments about the way he looked.

"The army hasn't done you any harm," Zooky said.

"It's the Chinese army that might do him some harm," I said, stupid again.

"Don't say that," Zooky said. "You don't want to jinx him."

"Was boot camp rough?" I asked. "What was it like?"

"It was stupid, but it wasn't bad. You get up at four-thirty, five minutes to get dressed and make your bed, then some faggot drill sergeant inspects and gives you a hard time. Something like that all day. They try to be a constant pain in your ass, but you wait them out."

"Did you ever have to do KP?"

"Everybody does KP."

"How's the food in the army these days?" Zooky asked.

"Steak every day, Zooky, except when we have lobster. Powdered eggs in the morning. All the beer you can drink."

"Powdered eggs?" I'd never heard of powdered eggs before.

"They serve beer in the army?" Zooky said.

"So did anything finally happen with you guys and the Fanwoods?" Dinnerman asked.

"Let me give you one piece of advice, boychik," Zooky said.

"Nothing much. Lately it's been real quiet," I answered.

"You don't never volunteer for anything. Nothing. That's the only rule."

"So you didn't even rumble with them?"

"More or less. Not really."

"Anyway," he said to Zooky, "I already volunteered for something. I took the Airborne."

"What does that do? You jump out of airplanes? You're a paratrooper?"

"I still have to finish jump school, Zooky." Dinnerman looked at me. "Did you hear anything about that nigger? Are they gonna burn him? Sometimes I think about him."

"What do you mean? What nigger?"

"The guy they locked up, you know, when they let me go, because of what happened to Florry O'Neill."

"I don't know. I haven't heard anything."

"I bet they're gonna burn that poor sucker. He doesn't even know what happened to him. One day he's sleeping with Schwarzschild's junk, and the next day he's headed for the chair."

"I guess I haven't been paying any attention," I said.

"They shoot people when they come down in a parachute. It's like a shooting gallery. You're just hanging in the air and pop pop pop." Zooky imitated aiming a gun through his blind eyes.

"We catch the bullets with our teeth, Zooky, and we spit them back."

"Yeah. You and Houdini," said Zooky.

"You're gonna jinx him, Zooky. Don't say anything like that."

"What jinx? You can't jinx a meshugenah like that."

So you couldn't call it a war between the Bullets and the Fanwoods. It was just a skirmish. It didn't even last through the winter. When it gets cold and the snow flies it's hard to think of fighting in the streets. Winter is the most relentless aggressor. Hitler made his troops go into Russia, and millions of Russians died, Jews and everyone, and then the winter came on the steppes, and Hitler's armies died there. They froze in Russia. Winter hit them like revenge, and that eventually drove the Führer into his bunker and the rest of the Nazis to Argentina. As crazy as Ryan might have seemed to us for wanting to fight, he wasn't crazy enough to make his Fanwoods fight on some frozen streets. Besides, everyone wore so many clothes in the winter that you couldn't land a good shot, even with a sledgehammer. By the time spring came around the whole mess seemed forgotten, part of the past.

Two big things happened around the block in April. One was that President Truman stood up to General MacArthur, the madman who wanted to invade China and kill a lot of Chinese people and a lot of Americans on the way. So he fired him. That was on April 11. On April 28 the other thing happened. The Bullets got their baseball uniforms with *Zooky's Confectionery* in big purple letters on the back. MacArthur made his stupid speech where he said, "Old soldiers never die, they just fade away." Just as long as you get rid of them, I thought. Everyone, especially Dufner, liked to make fun of that speech. "Old gym teachers never die," he said once to Kutzer, who was persecuting him. "They just eat rotten jockstraps."

As soon as the Bullets got their uniforms they put them on and paraded down Ft. Washington. When Barney saw us he had a conniption fit.

"I thought you were gonna let me sponsor you," he shouted, and leaned so far out over his magazines to see all of us we thought he'd fall onto the sidewalk. "I'm the one who's had to put up with you every day."

"Barney, you told me you didn't want to," I said. "You said it was a waste of money for you."

"Who said that? I never said such a thing. It's good publicity and you can write it off your taxes. You should have asked me."

We all marched into Zooky's with the uniforms on and filled up the whole store.

"What is it?" he asked.

"We've got the uniforms on, Zooky. With *Zooky's Confectionery* in big purple."

"It looks good. It looks great," said Zooky, and he started bouncing up and down on his side of the counter, like a kid.

"What looks good," said his wife, coming in from the little closet kitchen in the rear. "What are all of you doing here? What are these kids all doing here, these hoodlums? If this is a stickup I'll give you a stickup. What is this, *Zooky's Confectionery*, a joke? Zooky, what have they got on their shirts?"

"Mrs. Tits," Stames said, but luckily she didn't hear that. "In honor of the best egg cream in Washington Heights, we've decided to put your name on all our shirts."

"Yeah, and somewhere else too," said Frankie Dufner. "You want to see where else?"

"What is this honor? You can die from some stinking honor," she said. "Buy something, and then tell me about honor." She was smiling, though, like she couldn't help it.

"Boys," said Zooky. "I feel great. You look great. You'll win all your ball games in those uniforms."

We changed back into old clothes and went down to the river to practice. The uniforms were only for league games. At that practice Baldeen told us, or rather Sugarman, who was back in form, told us from Baldeen's mouth, that our first preleague game was going to be on May 3, afternoon, and it was going to be against the Fanwoods. The silence was enormous. Fanwoods had maybe been in the back of our minds, but nobody had talked or thought Fanwoods all winter, and we knew we were going to high schools out of the neighborhood, and the issue would disappear, so we were almost home free, and here they were right in our faces again because of stupid Baldeen.

"Why the Fanwoods?" I asked.

"You play baseball, you play hardball," Baldeen said himself, not trusting his deepest wisdom to the mouth of Sugarman.

"You've got tits for brains, Baldeen," said Stamatakis.

"Why the Fanwoods?" I asked Sugarman after practice. "There are a hundred teams we could play. Why can't we just forget about the Fanwoods?"

"Jack Ryan came to me himself. He spoke to Baldeen and asked for the game."

"So you just said okay?"

"They just want to play ball," Sugarman said. "Ryan seemed

okay to me. I met his sister."

"Great," I said. "So did I."

"I like her," said Sugarman.

"You like the Irish girls, Sugarman," Dufner said. "Why don't you find yourself a nice Jewish girl?"

Suddenly for me the ghost of Florry O'Neill seemed to settle on this whole conversation and make all the jokes strange. Sugarman didn't seem to mind. He had passed through it. He was turning into one of those people who could suffer a lot, and then forget it. His was a healthy attitude. It was just me. I couldn't forget Florry O'Neill, and that colored boy locked up because of it, to sit in the electric chair.

"Didn't you and Baldeen ever think that what the Fanwoods want to do is get us all down there so they can jump us," Zoo said.

"It wasn't like that, Zoo," said Sugarman. "They want to play ball."

"Yeah," said Grossman. "Old Bullets never die. . . ."

"They just quit the Bullets," Dufner added. "I'm quitting the Bullets. This is it. I'm a lover, not a fighter."

"You're not even a lover, Dufner," said Stames. "I talked to Audrey Wolfe."

"Yeah," said Grossman.

"Sit on these and rotate," said Dufner, lifting both his middle fingers.

*　　*　　*

So on the afternoon of May 3 once again the Bullets had to face the Fanwoods. Baldeen and Sugarman talked us into it. If we didn't play in this game, we couldn't play in any of the league games. Everyone showed up. Fourteen Bullets. Myself I thought okay. Play a game for Florry O'Neill. We got there early and started warming up, some calisthenics, some wind sprints, batting practice, infield drill, fungoes to the outfield. We all stopped when we saw it, like it was our mutual nightmare, that cloud of black jackets coming at us down the path of the park at Riverside Drive. We slowly moved closer together. A few of them in the front carried their baseball bats. Hubby ran over to our duffel and pulled out all our bats and distributed them to the members of the infield. I leaned on the bat he gave me and thought, not this, Jesus, not this.

When they got closer we saw that maybe they had actually come to play ball. They had baseball mitts, and were pounding their fists into the pockets. They looked as mean as ever when they walked onto the field, but they had actually come to play ball. They did nothing friendly, but stared at us like Ezzard Charles looking at Jersey Joe Walcott before a fight. They didn't seem to want to swing those bats at anything but a baseball. Ryan looked at me at one point, with a certain look of recognition that comes from some deep place you hold in common. I remembered that look once when I went to a party on the Bowery with the client I mentioned before who was an artist. She has since become famous herself, and has already sold all the paintings she could ever possibly paint in her life. She's hiding out in New Mexico now. That party was in the loft of another artist who was becoming famous fast, and he was living with Eva Hesse. It was the first time I saw her after I found out who she had become; and she looked at me, and it was a look that saw me and saw a little kid at the same time, just as I saw it in her. The room was full of New York people, all grown up, all holding glasses of wine, some of them not even New Yorkers, but from the Midwest or California or Italy, and Eva looked at me and put a finger to her lips, as if asking me to keep it a secret between us, our childhood together in Washington Heights. Somehow that look of Eva's brought Florry O'Neill to my mind, and the look Ryan gave me before the game, as if to say whatever was is over, and this is the next step.

There weren't many ballplayers among the Fanwoods. You could tell from the way they warmed up. Our infield had begun to look real snappy, but they stumbled around looking like they were trying to invent the game all over again. It made us feel like pros watching them. This was a cinch. This would be a piece of cake.

"Maybe we better not beat 'em," said Stames.

"Nah," said Sugarman. "We'll beat 'em."

Baldeen was sitting on his haunches and scouting them. He signaled for Sugarman to come over and squat down next to him, and then had a long whisper in his ear. Sugarman came back over to us.

"They got a couple of guys. A pitcher and a catcher who Baldeen says are really good." He pointed at two guys warming up in the outfield. "The pitcher's name is Christopoulos. He pitches for G.W."

"He's a Greek," Stames said in disbelief.

"And the other guy, Stein, is his catcher."

"Stein?" several of us said in unison. It could have been a German name, but it was probably Jewish, and on the Fanwoods. I met a great guy named Sean Golden once, and he was

Irish, and not even Jewish. The mayor of Dublin was Jewish for a while, too. And I found out later that Leopold Bloom, James Joyce's character, was supposed to be Jewish. So why not on the Fanwoods?

"He hits a long ball," Sugarman said.

"They're not even Fanwoods," said Mamoulian, "and they play high school ball."

"You want to tell them they can't play?" Sugarman said.

"What'll we do?" Mamoulian asked.

"We'll win," said Sugarman. "Schletzbaum is good. Stein has never faced him before, and they're both lefties."

"They always throw ringers in against us," Grossman said.

"That's 'cause we're good," said Sugarman. He turned to see Dufner walking across the field. "About time you got here, Dufner."

"I was waiting."

"Waiting for what?"

"To see if someone needed to call the police."

"Warm up, Dufner. The game's gonna start."

The game was more or less a pitcher's duel. I mean the outfielders could have gone to sleep, and I think Stames did once in right field. The only action was tossing the ball around the infield after Schletzbaum struck someone out. We didn't have a chance against this Christopolous either. He was so fast I'd still be waiting there for the pitch after it was in the catcher's mitt. And it was the first time we had ever really seen a sharp breaking curve. We were falling out of the batter's box until we realized what was going on.

We had two umpires. Baldeen called the game when the Fanwoods were at bat, and Ryan, who said he didn't like base-ball, but played football for the body contact and bone breaking, called them when we were up. He was really fair as an umpire; in fact, he always gave us the benefit of the doubt if the pitch was close. Not that it made any difference. Everyone was striking out.

The game was supposed to go seven innings, and in the top of the sixth it was still 0-0. Schletzbaum had walked one in the second and one in the fourth, but the Fanwoods couldn't touch him, though Stein connected for a couple of line drives foul. For a kid who was so fast Christopoulos had great control. Nobody got on base until Zoo worked him for a walk in the third, and then stole second to cause some excitement, but there were two outs, and of course I struck out on a curve ball that started in Connecticut and ended in South Jersey.

With one out in the sixth inning, Christopoulos connected for a clean single over second base. Bloustein, who had come to the team with Baldeen, and moved Zoo to left field, fielded the ball perfectly and held him on first. Schletzbaum struck out Kevin, who swung so hard that if he ever connected we'd say goodbye to the ball, or whoever was in its way. Stein was up next, swinging three bats in the on-deck circle. As soon as he stepped into the batter's box you could feel something charge up. Something horrible for us was going to happen. I walked up to the pitcher's mound to talk to Schletzbaum. Sugarman came in from short.

"Why don't we just walk this guy?" I said.

Schletzbaum looked at me as if I'd insulted his father.

"What do you think, Freddy? He ought to walk him, right? That red-headed kid up next can't hit."

"He's pitching. He knows better than we do. Anyway that red-headed kid is a righty, and Stein is a lefty. With a left-handed pitcher you don't pass a lefty to get at a righty."

"Play ball," Baldeen shouted from behind the plate. Baseball sense. I couldn't believe it, it sounded so stupid. Baldeen was the umpire. I couldn't consult with him. "Play ball," he shouted again.

"I don't give intentional walks," Schletzbaum said. I couldn't believe it.

"That's part of baseball," I said.

"Not the way I play it."

The first two pitches to Stein were wide, so I figured maybe he'd walk him anyway. Stein swung at the next pitch and pulled the ball right at me like a bullet and I stuck up my glove and even jumped a little, but three minutes after it was gone behind me, fouled down the right field line, called by Baldeen, and even verified by Ryan. 2 and 1. Stein swung and missed at the next pitch. It was beautiful to watch him swing, even when he missed. His swing was even and fluid, and his whole body was into it, and he followed through; I mean, he was the meaning of "follow through," the bat way behind him, his left knee bent to the ground.

The next pitch was a ball to make it 3 and 2. He'll walk him, I thought, and relaxed. I sighed with relief when I saw the pitch going wide, but Stein wasn't going to let that happen. He stepped almost across the plate to swing at that pitch, and lofted one so far into center field, and so high that it was out of sight. I could hear Mel Allen in my mind shouting "going... going...," and it was gone. Bloustein just watched it, and Zoo started after it, but stopped. Two days later it was probably still going. The score was two to zip. Schletzbaum struck out the next two, and we were up in the bottom of the sixth. And we were down 1, 2, 3, in the bottom of the sixth.

There was no more damage in top of the seventh, and we

were up again with Hubby, Schletzbaum, and the top of the
order with Zoo and then me, who batted second like Tommy
Henrich, in the unlikely case that I was needed. Seven innings
didn't seem to have tired Christopoulos at all. He struck Hubby
out easily. Schletzbaum would have loved to get back at him, to
be the first to hit him; but though he was a good pitcher he was
no hitter at all. He stared down Christopolous' face to intimi-
date him, but no luck; one foul tip, two balls, three strikes. He
was out. Grossman had his catching gear tied up together.
Hubby was collecting the bats to put them in the duffel. The
Bullets were ready to go home.

"What do you expect?" Hubby said to me, as he watched Zoo
step into the batter's box. "That guy pitches for George
Washington."

"They probably paid him," Dufner said.

"Still we should have won this game," I said. "They weren't
hitting Schletzbaum, except for Stein."

We shut up. Zoo for some reason still was in the middle of the
game, working Christopoulos. Greek against Greek. Christopoulos had him 1 and 2, but Zoo kept fouling him off, just stuck
out his bat and got a piece of the ball, and the count got to 3 and
2. I was half hoping he'd strike out, so I didn't have to make the
last out of the game. Christopoulos looked impatient. He threw
the last pitch wide, and Zoo trotted down to first base, bouncing
up and shouting, "Come on, Swanny. Let's get 'em back."

Now the game depended on me. Strike-out Swanson. I
hadn't seen the ball all day. Christopoulos looked at me as if the
idea of pitching to me bored him, as if I might as well give it up.
He wanted it over with right away, and that was why he got
pissed when Ryan called the first pitch I waited out a ball. He
kicked the dirt around the pitcher's mound. He might just

throw me something I could hit, I thought. He looked angry, and just a little tired suddenly. I looked down at Baldeen, coaching at third. He rubbed his left hand across his chest. That was the bunt sign. I couldn't believe it. I called time and stepped out of the batter's box and looked at Baldeen again. The bunt sign, for sure. His left hand across his chest. Two out, we're down by two runs, and he wants me to bunt. I couldn't believe it. Aside from the fact that of all things I hated to do in baseball, bunting was the worst of them, this didn't even make sense as strategy. Bunt with two outs, down by two? Zoo had a long lead off first. "C'mon Swanny," he was shouting. He was in the game. The other Bullets had stood up, and were watching, a little excitement rising even among those who had given up. The game was not over, as they said, until the last out. The bunt sign was on me. Christopoulos wound up, and pitched, and the ball was by me before I had even half-heartedly squared away. Baldeen called time and signaled me to meet him half way down the third base line.

"Are you playing baseball, or is this 'go fish'?"

"I think I can hit him, Baldeen."

"The bunt sign is on," he said, and walked back behind third.

I hated it. And to square away and face head on someone with a fastball and a curve like Christopoulos, that was craziness.

"Swanny babes, let's go," shouted Hubby. "Just put it down somewhere. They can't see it anyway." Someone grabbed Hubby and gagged him, but the excitement was still there, like the game had just started. That's baseball, with nothing happening the excitement grows. The next pitch was so wide I didn't even bother to square away. I looked down to third. Bunt. Why? I had to do it. I was playing for a team. We had this manager, who was supposed to know the best strategies. Even though I thought this was stupid I had to do it. I squared away and the pitch came down right at me. Curve, I thought. I felt it touch my bat, and then this incredible shock, like all the doors had slammed around my head, and everyone was shouting, "Run, Swanny. Go babes. Great bunt, Swanny." Before I even knew what had happened I was safe on first base, and Zoo was sliding into third, safe, and there was this throbbing in my head I couldn't believe. I put my hand up to my face and could feel it swelling. I had hit that bunt with my eye. It was a foul ball in the rule books, but no one had seen it, including me. Now Stames was up, the winning run at the plate, and you could see Christopoulos was a little shook with two men on base, and Stein waving at the outfield to send them deep. It was Greek against Greek again. It was the Trojan War.

"C'mon Stames. C'mon babes. Hit for the big boobs." The Bullets were all up and jumping by the bench. Zoo took his lead off third, and I, with my head throbbing a ton, took my lead off first. The eye that had bunted the ball was closing up. I didn't understand how I'd stayed on my feet, getting hit like that. But I guess I'd proved it enough times: hit me in the head and I'm fine. Christopoulos looked like he wished he'd never come to this game, as if he'd like the whole scene to disappear. A train went by on the tracks beyond the fence, and he waited for it to pass. I heard a small plane flying up the river but I couldn't see it. The train was gone, and Christopoulos toed the rubber, and went into his full windup. He kicked high in the air, and came down with everything he had left behind that first pitch he threw at Stames. I didn't see what happened because I finally spotted that small plane flying under the bridge. That was amazing. That was illegal. I vaguely heard the crack of the bat, and then there was silence, so I thought it was probably a strike, but suddenly the whole Bullet team roared. That ball was gone. Stames had done it. Before I started to move he was almost down to first base. Zoo trotted home. I held a hand over my eye and touched every base. I didn't believe it. We had won the game and only I knew the quality of that victory. This was the second time we had beaten the Fanwoods and both times it was with some kind of bunt.

"You laid that one down, Swanny. Great bunt," Sugarman said, slapping me on the butt on his way to shake hands with Stames. "That's what kept us alive. That's baseball." I couldn't take it. I went off and leaned against the fence, holding my eye, my back to the Fanwoods. I turned only because I felt this weird silence behind me. There were all the Fanwoods gathered in a bunch behind third base, and the Bullets standing by the first base line, watching to see what they would do.

"Maybe it was a mistake to beat them," I heard Grossman say.

"It's never a mistake to win," said Sugarman.

Hubby spotted me. "Swanny. Look at Swanny. What happened to your eye?"

"Jesus." They all came closer to look at me.

"Which one of them hit you?" Stames asked.

"Christopoulos," I said. I couldn't help it. Even then I was a sick joker.

"That Greek. He isn't even a Fanwood," Stames clenched both fists.

So suddenly that we all jumped, this noise burst out of the Fanwoods. "Two four six eight/who do we appreciate/the Bullets the Bullets—yeeeaaahhhhh!"

That shocked us. Everyone was silent for a long minute. We

were even embarrassed, because the etiquette of this situation was that the winning team cheered first. We hadn't even thought of it. We got into our little huddle and cheered, but I felt like it sounded weak by comparison.

The Fanwoods left the field first, and the Bullets followed. I never would have believed that everything could have ended so peacefully. I lagged behind, because I didn't really want them to see my eye. At a certain point there was Jack Ryan, watching some Chinese guys pulling crab traps out of the river.

"Swanson, come here," he shouted at me. "You think they really eat that shit, out of this slimy river?"

"They must," I said. "Maybe that's why they turn yellow." It was a nasty joke, and he liked it.

"Hey. You really used your head on that bunt," he said, and touched my swollen eye. He saw what happened, and he had been the ump, and he hadn't said anything.

"Why didn't you call it?" I asked.

"Listen, it wasn't my idea to get Christopoulos to pitch for us, or Stein. That was stupid. That was chickenshit. But I wanted to see if you guys could beat him. Big high school pitcher."

"Did you guys have to pay him to pitch for you?" That was me, Swanson, one too many questions.

"Baseball is a game," Ryan said. "No big thing."

"You never know," I said to him.

"I know you're still a punk," he said. "And you tell that little Jewboy, Sugarman, to lay off my sister." He raised a fist at me and left.

So there I was, Swanson, by the river, alone, swollen eye. I went over to where the Chinese guys were pulling out the crabs and squatted down by their straw baskets to watch. I could hear the crabs moving under the wet newspaper. One old man came over and touched my eye with his pinky and made a sucking sound.

"You eat these crabs?" I asked.

He pulled back the *Daily News* to show me.

"You eat these crabs?" I asked again.

He didn't understand me. "Two dollah," he said. "Mamma good."

If I'd had two dollars I would've bought them off him, just to scare my mother, and keep her from looking at my eye. I walked up to Haven Avenue by myself. All the Bullets were proud of that victory and thought it meant a great season for us in the Kiwanis. I was a little proud of it too; how it resolved things in a weird way, how I, pardon the bad joke, had used my head to bunt my way out of the traps of Washington Heights. Florry O'Neill, my love for you runs deep, deep as the river, that river of all our dreams that first astonished Henry Hudson. That game was a satisfaction. It gave all of us, especially the Bullets, a few months before they disappeared into high school, to live in Washington Heights, as if it was a place where you could live, like California, or Colorado.